DRIVING CRAZY TO THE FRONT DOOR

DRIVING CRAZY TO THE FRONT DOOR

STORIES

MICHAEL FOY

The stories, characters, and incidents in this collection are products of the author's imagination or used fictitiously, and any resemblance to actual people (living or dead), events, or locales is purely coincidental.

Prepared for the press by Alexander Hackett, Jennifer McMorran

Cover image: Alex Winchester, iStock
Cover design: Debbie Geltner
Layout: Daniel Ursache

Library and Archives Canada Cataloguing in Publication

Title: Driving crazy to the front door: stories / Michael Foy.
Names: Foy, Michael (Short story writer), author.
Identifiers: Canadiana (print) 20260162833 |
Canadiana (ebook) 2026016285X |
ISBN 9781773902043 (softcover) | ISBN 9781773902067 (PDF) |
ISBN 9781773902050 (Ebook)
Subjects: LCGFT: Short stories.
Classification: LCC PS8611.O94 D75 2026 | DDC C813/.6—dc23

Printed and bound in Canada

Legal deposit—Library and Archives Canada
and Bibliothèque et Archives nationales du Québec, 2026

We are grateful to the Canada Council for the Arts, the Canada Book Fund, and SODEC for their support of our book publishing program and to the Government of Quebec through the Société de développement culturel and the Programme de credit d'impôt pour l'édition de livres—Gestion SODEC.

Montreal
www.lindaleith.com

For Leo and Margaret, though darker now,
it is brighter than had you never been.

TABLE OF CONTENTS

THE POWDERMAN

SOME SAY YOU work better when someone watches you. I say horseshit. What I get is even more likely to screw things up, especially when it's Jerry LaDouceur staring over my shoulder. He tells people to call him Deuce, but no one does, and behind his back the guys call him Douche—because you can't make up your own nickname.

"We follow blast protocol here. Warning Signal. Blast Signal. All Clear. No one gets killed that way. So get out there and give it ten long pulls. Will, you should be good at that by now," Jerry says, pushing the column shifter into park.

He grabs the two-way radio, "All good down here. Green light. Starting blast protocol."

Jerry places the handheld back on its hanger.

"10-4," comes the response.

"Go, Will, go, go," Jerry tells me.

Jerry's our mechanic, the Pitt River Quarry know-it-all. He's short, with a shaved head and a neck bigger than my thigh. He's like a human plug, all thick and round and ready to stop things up. His arms, like ham hocks, rest on the truck's steering wheel. He wears his grease on his fingers and knuckles and has it smeared across his face like a QB's eye black. Jerry's always holding a cigarette, with the smoke winding around his head like he smolders, ready to ignite.

Competition for mine resources happens above and below ground—sure, there's the granite, but it's more than that. Jerry and Daniels fight for the better job, more money, and Daniels's wife Maria. They're mining for hatred. Once, Jerry choked Daniels out for sharpening drill bits. Daniels is local 168—wrong union, wrong job, and he was doing it in front of the wrong guy. Jerry told him to turn off the sharpener, twice, but Daniels just kept on givin 'er, thought he could ignore Jerry. Jerry reached up, put him in a half nelson, and dragged him from the machine.

"Bud," Jerry whispered in his ear, "that is my fucking livelihood."

Daniels, his face tomato-red, tugged at Jerry's forearm, even tapped at it with the palm of his hand—but Jerry wouldn't let up, and Daniels went limp. His steel toe boots fell together pigeon-toed before skidding over a length of chain and a triangular piece of scrap metal.

Jerry laid him out on the pea gravel like he was laying down one of his kids for an afternoon nap, tossing his yellow hardhat on the ground beside him.

"He'll wake up in a minute or so," Jerry said, "with a brand-new take on the division of labour."

All that happened two weeks ago.

When things go wrong at the quarry, you can't exactly call up the labour relations board and file a complaint.

Right now, I'm a nothing. I get the crap jobs, and someone has to watch and give me all the advice I can handle: *No, no, no that goes there... Never, never start here, Will... Make sure that you're standing at least this far back before you put the power on... Why would you do that? Were you even listening to what I said?* But still, I wonder who watches the guys at the top.

In three weeks, I start training for my blasting ticket. Daniels is the powderman now, our explosives expert, but he's taking off for Alberta and the almighty oil fields. At lunch we hear all about it.

"They gotta drill those wells. Am I right, boys? We should all go," he rubbed his thumb across his fingertips, "that's where the money moves."

"It's a lateral move, Daniels, a lateral move," Jerry said. "And a total waste of time."

"Ya, well fuck you, Jerry, none of this matters to you anyways, all you do is fix our shit when we break it. Any jackoff can do that. But if I don't show up for work tomorrow, and there's no blast, you're sent home. *You're* a fucking lateral move, Jerry; your whole life is one big lateral move."

I listened to them argue and ate my ravioli, swiping a slice of buttered bread along the lid of the can for that last smear of thick red sauce. I washed it all down with a half-carton of Tropicana orange juice, buried my hand in a bag of sunflower seeds, filled one cheek, walked over to the front step of the dry, sat down and spat out shells.

There was a huge truck tire outside the dry turned on its side, the centre filled with black earth and a half dozen tomato vines growing all thick and green. Daniels has a green thumb, and the beefeaters are red and plump, ready to be eaten. When you work at an open pit mine it's easy to imagine some place better, and whenever I had a moment, that's what I did. And lately, I looked at the guys I worked with—will that be me one day? They're worn out, expired, like an old singer in a rock band. For my backup, I applied to teacher's college. A two-year program. The classes start in the fall. The money isn't great, but how much money do you really need? Besides, summers off, that's gotta be worth somethin'. The academic counsellor at UBC said, "It's a chance to work with tomorrow."

My older brother always said I would make a good teacher.

"Don't get stuck at the mine, Will; it grinds away at you, till there's nothin' holding you up but the powder."

"Yeah, but I like construction. At the end of the day, I can look back and see what I've done. The bags lifted, holes dug, and boulders blasted. The crushed rock at the end of each conveyor is used for roads, dock pilings, and ballast. I helped put it there."

After I'd said that, I realized how stupid it sounded, because you could put just about anything that anyone does in that sentence and act all proud—like you're doing your piece for the greater good—but how do you really know? Is laying a sheet of asphalt over the ground a good thing? Is covering the planet in pavement? Truth is, I'm not sure what I wanna do.

I fumble with the door handle before I get out of the pick-up and into the summer heat. It's August and my T-shirt and jeans are brittle under a layer of sweat and caked-on dust. Standing here at the powder magazine I can see the Pitt River down below, winding its way through fields of potatoes and corn and into Pitt Lake, resting at the base of Thompson Mountain. It's Friday, and at shift's end I'll swim on my back in those blue-grey waters. I'll get the Irish Spring and the bottle of Head and Shoulders from the glove box, and I'll lather off that layer of dust, I'll loosen the gravel in my hair. I pull the air horn over and over: seven-eight-nine-ten-warning signal, because it gets me closer to jumping into that water.

This is Daniels's last blast. If I make powderman, it means going up the pay scale, and then bring on the overtime. When you run the blast, you're important: they need you. No more boulder hopping carrying a jackhammer, no more hoofin' bags of ANFO, because you're King Shit on Shit Mountain. No one screws with the powderman; without him, nothing happens. No boulders to feed the crusher, no oversize to re-pile and blow again. All the front-end loaders, the dumpers—parked, a giant row of unused Tonka toys. The two scows sit empty too, resting high up on the water, bumping the pilings. Without the powderman the Quarry stops dead.

When it goes, this blast will blow the face clean off bench three, but I know it's the faces in upper management that Daniels wants changed. He's fed up. He has two boys at home aged six and eight. Maria is expecting and she's getting on his case about how little money's coming in.

"Maria talks about money like it's water shootin' up from the ground that I can catch in a bucket," Daniels said. "She's expecting alright—expecting me to become a millionaire."

Money's only part of the problem. Maria's had it with Daniels and his drinking—and the coke. With each gram coming in at $100, Daniels can't continue on that slippery slope; eventually, he'll go down. He spends most of his time at the Gillnetter drinking beer and snorting his wages in a rolled up twenty. It's like he's holed up in an army bunker, surrounded by barbed wire and deep trenches, and his wife and kids are the enemy. He just needed to roll out a table map, hold each corner down with a glass of beer, and explain his plan of attack. *You won't get me outta here alive.*

After a couple of trips into the Gillnetter bathroom Daniels came to life, with all the energy and optimism of a caged man. He knew he could talk here. He was safe at the pub. He told us that the block of blue granite would soon run dry and we'd all be collecting UI. He was afraid of something, but nothing we could see. According to Daniels you had to have a Plan D: a way out of a place that had completely caved in. But we knew that granite was good for another half-century.

Last Saturday Jerry came to the Newton Inn at two in the afternoon. Daniels and I had been drinking beer, playing pool, and watching the dancers spin on the pole for a couple hours. Daniels was half in the bag when Jerry showed up. Jerry stared at the ground as he walked in from the too-bright sunshine. His brow was furrowed: it created this long ripple of skin on his forehead, like he was trying to sprout horns. Jerry circled the pool table and grabbed a handful of Daniels's shirt, knocking a pack of Craven As to the floor.

"Your red Chevelle's in the goddamn parking lot," Jerry said, pushing, and pulling Daniels in time with the words—you could hear Daniels's collar tear. "Your two boys sittin' out there in the back seat too scared to get outta the car. It's summer for Christ's sake!"

Daniels made an arm circle and came down hard with his elbow on Jerry's forearm and broke his grip. "Whatever, douche, if I'm losing, let me lose," Daniels said. "That's what I'm here for."

He stepped on his pack of cigarettes on his way back to the table, lined up his shot and struck the cue ball, sending the balls clacking all over, but nothing dropped. His stretched shirt collar hung low from his neck, like a slackened noose, and revealed patches of inflamed skin on his collarbone.

"You gonna get out there or what?" Jerry asked.

The kids are Maria's insurance policy. Daniels has to take the boys on any weekend trips from the house, so she can be sure of a sober return. So much for that.

But two weekends ago, it was Jerry who was too drunk to drive home, and the bartender asked me to give him a lift. When we turned on to the King George, Jerry let it all spill, even broke down crying, said he loved Maria, and she had a right to be happy. She told Jerry she's ready to walk. She wants a family again.

With Daniels back at the table and into his game and me on my fourth beer, I approached Jerry. "Where were you all afternoon? Shouldn't you be thanking Daniels for getting the kids outta the house?"

Jerry turned to face me, "Pissing with the big dogs now, eh? Worry about yourself, this doesn't concern you."

He scratched the top of his head, the skin streaked with nail marks.

That was when Jonah, Daniels's eight-year-old walked into the bar, all red-faced and sweaty. His brown hair hung an inch above the green felt on the pool table. He lifted his head up to look at Jerry.

"Can you please tell my dad that Jason got sick in the back seat. He's not feeling too well."

Jonah turned and stared at the lady on stage with his mouth open.

Daniels left after that.

For the next blast, Daniels wanted all the holes filled with an eight-inch collar.

"When I stand next to any hole, I should see ANFO at the top, and not just those holes furthest from the face. You hear me? All the holes."

I knew it meant overspray, boulders—breadbox-sized and floating through the air. Once airborne they would reach the weigh scale trailer. Guaranteed. And that's where the big wigs are having their annual production meeting—one Audi, two Beamers, a Merc, and a chromed-out F-250 towing a trailer with two blue and red

Sea-Doos—all parked way down below bench three and within range. They bought the things we couldn't.

After last year's meeting I had to rinse the dust from their cars with a garden hose. There'd be no rinsing today. The way Daniels has this blast set up, they'll need a front-end loader to get at their cars.

"No raise in three years, means no fucking ride home," Daniels said. "Walk a mile in my shoes, boys."

The sun lit up his curly blond hair and his sun-flecked skin. He wore a T-shirt that read: *Based On A True Story*. He smiled, and when he did you saw all of his teeth and it made you wanna smile too, no matter what he was sayin'.

"Better to burn bright and hard, then fade out!" Daniels yelled.

"Whoa D-man," I said. "The less I know the better."

Walking the air tracks along the top edge of that cliff face, it took us two weeks to drill ninety holes forty feet deep, imbed blasting caps in the gel sticks and drop 'em down, without letting go of the orange cord. Then we filled each hole with ANFO and topped it off with sand and gravel. After that, we tied all the lines together like the grid system on an archaeological dig. These past two weeks, while Daniels was planning a way out, I was planning a way in. He wanted to make a statement: *his swan blast*. And I'm in on it whether I like it or not. And now, Daniels is crouched down, waiting to plunge the handle on the shot exploder. *Zing*. And send 500 volts travelling the line, triggering a blast that will pulverize the granite cliff face.

"Okay, Will. One minute of short pulls."

I pull the chain on the air horn in one-second bursts: fifty-seven, fifty-eight, fifty-nine, sixty. Blast Signal.

I see the dust cloud before the car. It's Maria driving the red Chevelle and tearing up the gravel. She's done it before, swinging the car into the parking lot, ignoring the heavy machinery and other dangers. She flies past and hits the first bench going about 50km. Her car zigzags up the switchbacks like a spark chasing the fuse. She reaches bench two before I even make it back to the cab.

"That's Maria and the kids!"

"Jesus," Jerry says starting the truck. "Get on the two-way!"

I grab the handheld and press the call button. "Daniels! Daniels! Stop! Stop the blast!"

I listen. Nothing.

Earlier in the day I peeled the coil of line off for the shot exploder, so I know Daniels is about 100 yards back from the blast site, and there is no way he can see Maria flying up that gravel road. No way. Jerry was supposed to secure the swing gate at the mine entrance. *No visitors allowed.*

If you've ever watched a blast detonate, you know that you can see it a fraction of a second before you hear it. The farther away, the greater the lapse between the movement and the sound reaching your ears. It's a brief look into the future: a stutter in real time. Jerry and I are on the gravel road and starting our ascent to bench three, Jerry is hammering away on the horn but all we see is the explosion, the expansion of that peninsula of rock up and out, marked by little grey and black plumes of dust and smoke, like handfuls of chalk powder thrown into the air. *Boom.* A thunderous rumble pulses through everything and creates a giant dust cloud that moves slowly toward us, so thick you can't see your hand in front of your face. Jerry hits the brakes, and everything slows. The dust cloud hides the falling rock, pieces of it land at different times like the first drops before heavy rain. Some stones hit the ground, others rat-a-tat-tat off the hood of the truck. It lasts for a minute, until all the rock has fallen from above, and we hear nothing. Not even a bird or a scream.

ALL THE LITTLE THINGS

STILL STANDING on the counter, holding his cereal bowl to his chest, James shifts his gaze.

"Dad, have you seen someone die?"

Reggie stops stirring his coffee, lifts and drops the spoon. *Clink.*. "You know I don't like you climbing up there."

Seven-year-old James Seeley jumps down. Blond hair, like broken bits of straw, frames his face. Reginald Seeley slides the carafe back onto the warmer. Scratching the top of his shaved head, he flips off the switch.

Reggie wears a blue correctional officer's uniform; his duty belt is fitted with a flashlight, handcuff case, and key clips. He's used to having everything within reach.

"What are you having, son? Shreddies? Mini Wheats? Or your fave, Cap'n Crunch?"

Usually, distraction works, but James is too old now.

"Cap'n Crunch and the big spoon. *Have* you, Dad? Have you ever?"

Reggie blinks several times. Correctional Officers are taught to mask emotion. Feel it and let it go. Never wear it on your face. Reggie looks down at his boy's bare feet, at the arches, high like his mother's. He pours Cap'n Crunch into James's bowl, and two of the little orange squares escape and drop to the floor. James slides from his chair and crawls under the table after them.

"Careful, Dad, you might crunch them with your boot."

"Get up here."

But James keeps talking from down there. "Donnie Corgan said you help them die. Is it true?"

"Donnie Corgan's older than you, isn't he?"

"Grade Four. He showed me on his iPhone, all sorts of pictures of the people at the prison, all dressed in orange. What's a strap-down team and why do you hold their ankles?"

Reggie thinks that Steve Corgan, Donnie's dad, must have had his head entirely up his ass during that part of the training. All guards *must* maintain a code of silence about the execution team with outsiders—code blue.

Reggie misses Carol. His wife would have intervened here, saying something like, "Hurry up and finish that cereal, let's get you ready for school," and ushered James away from the table, while tucking his hair behind his ear. And James would listen. Carol would have been there after school, with a kiss for the top of his head and wanting to talk. She gave James all the little things he needed, but died two years ago. Reggie remembers how he always sat in the chair next to the hospital bed with his legs crossed at the ankle, while James slept beside her. The tumours kept spreading. Some nights, she read his favourite stories, using all of her wacky voices—slow to build suspense and quick on the action.

There was a futility in the IV drip, the injections, and the monitoring of vitals; in James being told he had to move from the bed, and the sound of the privacy curtain's slide along the rod—opening and closing for the nurses, the bed bath and plastic food trays. Everyone was doing so much to keep her alive. But her weight kept dropping, until she was only bony cheeks. When she passed away, within twenty-four hours, her body was moved to the funeral home, and Reggie was left with too many what-ifs. What if he had opted for Critical Illness Insurance? What if that clinical trial they refused could have stopped the spread?

"Later, James. We'll talk tonight. Get up off the floor and finish your cereal. I poured the milk. It'll get soggy."

"Cap'n Crunch never gets soggy."

James sits back in his chair, scoops up a spoonful, crunching and slurping at the biscuits bathed in orange milk.

"Remember, son, no bus home today. We have a meeting with Mrs. Redding. I'll see you out front of the school—got it?"

"Got it."

"Put your lunch in your backpack. That school bus ain't waitin' for no one."

They stand at the entrance of the Blue Valley Trailer Park waiting for the morning school bus. This is new to Reggie's routine. He hates the wait, the lack of control. They face the rows of empty concrete pads in the lower half of the trailer park, each with a picnic table and a grey post bubbled by a hydrometer. The evenly spaced posts are like an army of robots awaiting command. Most of the summer campers are gone, their RVs migrated to winter storage. The grass gleams in the dew and the day's quiet, except for the sound of tires on gravel when the park super drives past on his golf cart, giving the horn a couple taps.

"Mornin', gents."

"Mornin'."

The school bus rolls up next and the driver yanks the silver handle, springing the door and popping the flashing stop sign into place. Reggie follows his son up the steps.

He scans the passengers while the diesel engine chugs in the background, and he sees every face but Donnie's.

"Hey, Mel," he says to the driver. "Just looking for little Donnie."

"Didn't get on."

"Oh, okay. James won't be on the after-school bus. I'm picking him up."

Reggie's about to get off when two kids in the front row notice his uniform: the duty belt, the badge, the vacant radio hanger, and the wide brim on his grey trooper hat.

"Mister, you got a gun?"

"Hey, you only carry a gun when you're on tower duty or escorting prisoners off prison grounds."

"That's sick!"

Reggie steps off, the bus drives away. He takes his Ford F-250 to the staff parking lot at the Washington State Prison, takes his duffle bag from the truck bed and checks his watch: 7:43. He's missed the morning briefing. He flashes his ID, and they buzz him in. He grabs the briefing summary from his mail slot, checks out keys, a radio, and rubber gloves. He scans the bullet points:

- scissors found in cell 404 confiscated and removed
- barbed wire near the south fence parking lot, second to last stall—bent, unable to straighten by hand
- two Charlie seven lost one hour of Rec for talking during quiet time

- Tom Wilkie's retirement party. Early release for good behaviour! The Green Lantern Pub this Tues 7pm.

Reggie walks into the Level One observation office to relieve Officer Corgan.

"Okay, Seeley, all your equipment's here. You got an upper and a lower coming out today. Head count of eighty-nine. Your run-arounds are Thompson out of two and Moralez out of six. And today *is* Wednesday, so you *do* have uniforms."

Steve Corgan hands the clipboard to Reggie, who slams it on the desktop.

"What the hell is your problem?"

"What?"

"You gotta rein Donnie in. He's showing James all sorts of shit online. Donnie told him I'm on the strap-down team. On the strap-down team, for Chrissake!"

"Look, Seeley, I got enough problems right now. Raising the kids is Lenora's job."

"Yeah, well, James is nonstop. And how does Donnie know so much anyway?"

"Google *Washington State Executions*—I dare yuh. You can see it all right there on Wikipedia. There have been seventy-eight executions since 1904, last meal, final words—the whole nine. So when Donnie asked me if I killed any of those men, I said, 'Damn right we did, two criminals, and we got eight more to go.'"

"Get rid of the cellphone. He's in Grade Four."

"Lenora wants it to keep track of him. Our kids will find out eventually. Is that what's got you so riled up?"

"Maybe that's it."

"You know what they called it before it was capital punishment?" He picks up a pencil from the desk and rubs the tip with his thumb. "Judicial homicide. Kinda points the finger at someone else. And these drugs are all screwy, too, you know it, you remember how Cal was. I say we get back on the grid and just zap 'em."

It was true. After injecting sodium pentothal, Cal Thomas coughed and heaved for close to thirteen minutes, struggling to breathe, his left eye slightly open, and staring out at the world. Thirteen minutes was long, when you're trying to be merciful. Then the physician pinched his right arm before injecting the pancuronium bromide, and Cal's right hand shook as if his bird tattoo wanted to flutter from his wrist. The physician had motioned for Reggie to tighten the strap. With the final injection of potassium chloride, Cal's index finger began to twitch, it was the only part of his body free to move, and it pointed at everyone in the room. The EKG was silent, no longer captured the impulses from Cal's upper and lower chambers.

Reggie says, "There's something wrong with the whole operation when we're the only ones walking in and walking back out again."

"Tell James you have a minor role, two leather straps and a pair of buckles. It amounts to nothin'. We're silent actors."

"Silent actors, my ass, and maybe that's the problem. They never ask how I feel about wheelin' away a body."

But Reggie wants to tell Corgan how often he squeezed Cal's forearm through the bars. How over his seventeen years of imprisonment Cal was a big part of his daily routine. That magnetic chessboard and all those matches, their moves exchanged on a lunch tray napkin.

"When I play," Cal often said, "I live so many lifetimes."

On execution day, as Reggie was buckling him in, Cal nodded, eyes closing slowly, as if to say, "It's okay, what you will do to me."

James is sitting on a blue bench next to the school office, waiting for his father.

"I told you to meet me *outside*," Reggie says approaching from the hall.

"I know, but Mrs. Redding asked me to wait here."

"Hello, Mr. Seeley," Mrs. Redding says, coming from the office. "Why don't we go into the conference room across the hall?"

Mrs. Redding walks back to the staff room.

"Mr. LeGarry, let's get started."

She turns back to Mr. Seeley.

"I invited Mr. LeGarry, our school counsellor."

"Fine with me."

"James," Mrs. Redding says in her soft voice, "we need you to wait out here, while we talk to your dad. After that, we can invite you in. Is that okay?"

"Yes."

"Here," Mr. LeGarry says, walking past James and placing a small box on the bench. "I know you love Star Wars LEGO; see if you can build this one for me."

James stares at the X-wing fighter, rattling the box.

"Cool."

Mrs. Redding leads the men into the conference room, leaving James on the blue bench. In the room, the blinds are closed; a long boat-shaped table takes up most of the space. A muffled whistle and shoes squeaking on the gym floor can be heard through a wall.

"Please," Mrs. Redding says, "take a seat. Thanks for coming, sir. We have some concerns about James and his schoolwork. His journal entries have us worried. As you know, James is still developing his writing skills, but his drawing is quite detailed for a boy his age. Mostly, he sketches death and dying."

She opens the journal to a page marked with a pink sticky and spins the book to face the father.

"And this content is certainly not related to anything we have covered in our curriculum."

Reggie examines the drawing. Most of the white space is filled. It is the interior of a room, and a lemon-coloured light fixture hangs from the ceiling. Several men, sketched in brown and black crayon, and drawn with heavy eyebrows, big noses and tiny mouths, stand around a woman lying prone on a table. Each person straps part of her body—left leg, right leg, left arm and torso, right arm and torso, head. The woman on the table has Xs for eyes. Reggie flicks his fingers across the drawing, knocking away bits of pink eraser. "Kil all her!" is scrawled into a word balloon with a black marker.

Reggie removes his trooper's hat, turning it upside down on the table. The sweatband is moist, and a stain marbles the liner.

"Mr. Seeley, would you like a glass of water?" Mrs. Redding asks.

"I'm fine."

Reggie draws a long breath, exhaling through his nose and crossing his arms.

"Mr. Seeley, we're worried. We know that Mrs. Seeley passed away about—"

Reggie raises his hand.

"Mrs. Redding. I'm not sure what to say," he says, tapping the picture with his index finger. "It's not right for my boy to be drawing pictures like this here."

Mr. LeGarry says, "Well, Mr. Seeley, we think James might be experiencing what they call complicated grief—"

Again, Reggie raises his hand.

"Look, mister, I appreciate your concern, but I'm not the one... I mean, I'm not. You see, Carol took care of James when it came to his schooling."

The conference room door clicks. A thin white line appears at its edge. Everyone turns, and the door swings open as if pushed by an unseen force. James runs in and dives under the table like he's jumping from the edge of a swimming pool.

"James," Reggie says. "Come out from under there, son."

"I heard," James sniffles. "It's not fair to look at my stuff."

"I see," says Mr. LeGarry. "Come out, bud, so we can sort this out."

Reggie pushes his chair out, peering under the table. His left hand trembles.

"Damn it! James Andrew Seeley, don't make me crawl in there to get you."

James is looking out at all the action around the table, the moving legs and feet, chairs on rollers. They're coming for him. He moves to the centre of the table. It's a chase, and he's got a hiding spot.

Mrs. Redding's voice is softer than the others.

"Honey, we were just about to invite you in. Come on out, sweetheart, so we can talk."

James rubs his eyes. His breathing picks up and blood moves to the surface of his skin, flushing his face. His Dad pushes chairs away, circling the table, looking underneath for a way to get at him. Tears roll from his eyes, his nose drips, and the more he wipes, the more slime smears across the back of his hand.

Mrs. Redding and Mr. LeGarry hunch over and look at James between chair and table legs. Reggie moves closer, and from his stomach he lunges, but James moves right and he misses. Reggie tries again, this time he clamps onto his son's right ankle and shuffles backward on all fours, dragging James out.

"Leave me alone! You took Mama like this. Because, because Donnie Corgan showed me. And you're in trouble now!"

Reggie lets go.

The boy dashes over to Mrs. Redding, who kneels, wrapping him in her arms. The shame of hearing the accusation introduces a silence to the room.

"I think it best if we end this," Reggie says.

Mrs. Redding nods, wiping James's nose with a Kleenex. With her hand at his back, she guides him closer to his dad. James spins to stand further away.

Reggie reaches for his son's hand and, holding it firmly, he pulls him closer, and realizes again how small it is. The fingers barely long enough to interlock with his. He puts his trooper hat back on his head and they leave the conference room.

Basketball practice is over, and the players are at the far end of the hall taking turns jumping and trying to touch the exit sign with one finger. The hall echoes with, "Sweet! You got this!"

Outside, rain and darkness fall from the clouds broiling across the sky. Reggie and his son walk to the truck. Despite his grip on James's shoulder, Reggie feels it all slipping. His whole life. Fatherhood. Everything. Every damn thing.

The musky smell of wet cedar drifts in from a clump of trees at the edge of the lot. Reggie opens the passenger door and lifts James into the booster, moves around to the driver's side, opens it, drops his hat on the seat and gets in. He puts the key in the ignition and turns off the radio. He leans back, pressing his fingers to his eyes and rubbing circles. Reggie's tears soften the edges, making the windshield swell and recede. He wipes his eyes on his sleeve and fixes his gaze on the odometer—the digits come into focus, ready to count his next move.

FORBIDDEN SPACES

Scccccratch. She puts the arm to rest, and the record stops. Then—to stamp it in—she presses the LEGO-sized power button. And with that, something great is lost. My musical solace is over. Well, sort of.

Mom's no Dr. Dre, but she likes her profanity.

"Get up! That little bitch stole my lighter. I know I had it the last time she was here. We sat right there," she points at the chesterfield, "and smoked *my* cigarettes. Next time I look for it—gone, and so was she—that's no small fucking coincidence."

Standing in a housecoat and slippers, holding an unlit cigarette, Mom places her tumbler of iceless and cokeless rum on the coffee table.

"Okay, okay," I say. "I'm moving, I'm moving, *relax*."

I lift my feet and head from the armrests, get up and move. I'm a spectator backing away from a street brawl. She scans the couch, wedges a hand into the crack between dark foam cushions, and slides it down like a chisel plough through soil.

Her eyes bug.

"Wait a minute... wait a minute."

Only to pull out three Life Savers welded to a nickel—all covered in cat hair.

Sherry Black has eight brothers and sisters, but we know little about them. In our neighbourhood, when anything goes wrong, is stolen, broken or missing, she's the prime suspect: guilty until proven innocent. Put out an APB, call *America's Most Wanted*, position the sound guy and roll cameras. Walk the streets and gather interviews from neighbours and family friends—anyone who knew Sherry before the stealing spree. I mean, c'mon, she would need a double-door garage to store it all.

Mom's derision pours out when Sherry isn't around, sloshing and splashing onto everyone. I don't understand. If you're angry with someone, shouldn't you tell *them,* I mean direct, face to face. Why should I have to listen to the bitching, the moaning, and the demands? Besides, I know where this rant is heading: to the Holy Grail, straight for The King himself. You know, the skinny one, before he got all drugged up and fat. The boy from

Tupelo—innocent and beautiful, like a fresh blade of grass.

Four months ago, a piece of Elvis Presley went missing: the 45 with "Blue Suede Shoes" and "Tutti Frutti" on the B-side. It was a birthday gift from my Dad, back when my parents started dating. He gave her the record the night before the big show: *Elvis Presley Live at Empire Stadium. Starring in Person. Price $1.50.* He still has her ticket stub.

Elvis took a train north from Seattle and then a green Cadillac. He sat in the back seat wearing a gold jacket when he pulled into the Empire parking lot, the stage before the stage. My old man said Vancouver was the only time Elvis left the U.S. to perform. What was he afraid of? Jet-black hair greased tight to his head, like fresh glaze on a candy apple. He carried his wristwatch with his fingers like he was about to toss it all away: the fame, the money, the women. Mom and Dad were tucked into folding stadium seats a mile away; they were still nicknames, weaved fingers, and moving closer.

Dad said the whole concert-performance-teenage-mania thing was new. Listening to him, I felt mostly sorry for the security team. At the start of the show, there was an entire football field, a chain-link fence, and a line of concert staff, air cadets, and police officers between 26,000 fans and The King. No one will rush the stage. "Got it? Got it." I bet my parents felt safe; thought they could sit back and watch the show, the start of an easy ride.

Ever see teen girls hopped up on infatuation and lust for The King of Rock 'n' Roll? They went all out, a little like Roger Bannister on the final leg of the Miracle Mile, but maybe not. You see, they were fuelled by something else. They ducked and weaved, even climbed and crawled, in-between legs, to get closer to Elvis—basic training for concert goers. Nothing would get between them and the King, least of all a chain-link fence or a bunch of air cadets.

Their mission, their primary goal: to see Elvis up close, real close, so close you could smell his Hai Karate after-shave and crawl through open lips and teeth and get to the back of his mouth and feel the sound waves leave his vocal cords on the way out to all those frenzied ears. They shredded that security line like government documents at the White House, the chain-link fence, and most of the grass field, too. Then, what mattered more than the scrambling, bashing, and desperation of it all, was telling someone that you were there. To wave that ticket stub and say that you saw The King of Rock 'n' Roll shake his ass and gyrate his hips all over stage. He's a fish on dry land. "And I was this close"—holding your hands two feet apart.

Elvis *was* right there, fingers snapping, legs bouncing, pouring his heart into that Unidyne microphone. He was standing alone atop a sound wave about to come crashing down on everyone. He started with "Money Honey," followed by "That's Where Your Heartaches Begin," "Hound Dog," and finished with "Jailhouse Rock." It lasted twenty-two minutes. Though it was brief, the fans could only stand there and love him harder. Then, in the faces of the round-the-clock screamers, above which you could barely hear the music, Colonel Parker, his manager, put a hand to his mouth and yelled at Elvis, "It's not safe, son. Get off the damn stage!" Elvis dropped the mic and then his jacket on a bodyguard's shoulders. The screaming mob chased that guy to the Cadillac. So Elvis ran through the parking lot alone, his black shirt flapping all the way to his dressing room. Pretty slick, huh? "For your information, Elvis has left the stadium. Please, go home."

When Mom looks for that record, you think she's misplaced the Hope Diamond or something. Her face changes, and she looks beyond you, fixating on an object in the distance; a sunrise or children laughing or something even more beautiful. Whatever you say doesn't matter. Of course, she nods and goes through the motions, but she's not listening, not really. You should hear her.

"Where did I listen to ... under a magazine ... when did I ... you sure that you didn't take it over to ... must be somewhere ... last time I had it your father was here ... "

Wherever that record is, would it remain there, hidden—undisturbed in some dark corner—just out of reach? Then no one could ever hear those silky-smooth tones again, because once you heard his voice you wanted more, like milkshake through a straw.

"That little bitch, she's probably listening to that record right now and using my lighter to smoke her Export As."

Well, I'm about to find out, because I'm going to her place. If Peters would just hurry up and get here. Peters lives next door. Right now, he is mowing the lawn, taking out the garbage and doing whatever else his mom wants before he gains clearance for an unescorted leave of the prison grounds.

I'm trapped, too, as Mom pours drink three. Maybe she thinks the search, and the drama, especially the drama, will draw attention away from the shadow Dad left. She doesn't want to talk about it. Dad said it was "just temporary, just a few weeks, buddy, and before ya know it, I'll be right back here to make your life miserable again." That was four months ago. I haven't seen him since. Besides, my dad had it all ass-backwards. I'm more miserable now than ever.

But I think I know why he left. A while back, I woke to my parents battling it out in the kitchen. It reached a certain level, a certain back and forth that I heard a lot. I remember their conversation from that night.

"Who's Mitch Fowler?" my dad asked. "Is he the one who runs the Camera Shop on Fraser Highway?"

Mom walked over and closed my bedroom door. I climbed out of bed and crawled to the register. On my stomach, with one ear on the cold grate, I heard their voices through the vents as if they were standing next to me.

"Yeah. He's a photographer. Just a friend," Mom said.

"Just a friend, eh? Well, for the third week in a row, Joe Linton along with everyone else at the pub saw you two together," he said. "And everyone could tell it wasn't a business meeting. Do you think I'm *that* stupid?"

"Wait, wait. Tom. Let me—"

"Maybe you could remind the prick that he took our family portrait. Our family fucking portrait."

I heard a bang on the kitchen table, a door slam—quick steps across the sidewalk, and the Buick rolling down the drive. He was outta here.

"Jeremy," my mom says now. "I think I see Peters out there."

"Yesss."

Even Mom calls him Peters. Who names their son Ogilvie? There should be a government name bureau, with an official Latin title like the Appello Magistrate, to screen every prospective child name. "Thomas, check. Andrew, check. Ogilvie? What the ...? Okay, get the parents on the phone ASAP. This is a Code Three violation."

I lost count of the number of times Peters scrapped with some kid at school because they said his name in a high-pitched tone while tipping their head from side to side. "Ooooogelveeee!" He usually lost the fight, which made it even worse, but over time he got better—faster,

I guess. He learned to throw punches high and hard, and the name-calling stopped.

There he is, at the foot of my driveway with his skateboard, wearing short pants meant to be long pants that barely cover his chubby frame. His long blond hair is one length, so you have a hard time seeing his face. He constantly whips his head back to see better, but he's not a supermodel or nothing, just a chubby kid, with a funny name and long hair.

"Hey, Peters, where's the flood?"

"Ha. Ha. I don't have a clothes budget like you, Saunders."

We have big plans. When you're our age, everything you try on your own seems big, at least bigger than you or your parents or anything else in your measly little life. We're heading for Lawson's. Tom Lawson owns a farm on the corner of Johnson and Serpentine. Well, he used to own it; some developer snatched it up like they did every other scrap of land around here. After Lawson's wife died, he held out, wanted to keep the farm, but it was too much work, so he had to sell. This is our last trip to the farm before they knock it all down.

We have another problem: old man Lawson owns a salt gun. Kaleb Whitby got hit with it two months ago. It was part of a dare. According to Kaleb, who's now the neighbourhood expert, if you're more than thirty feet away, then you have little to worry about, but any closer and it can do damage. Kaleb made it to the barn door before Lawson reached for his gun, then on to the garbage cans at the end of the gravel driveway before he took a shot right in the ass. Lawson, barking after the recoil, "Get off my land! Farmers feed cities, ya little bastard!" The blow knocked Kaleb onto his stomach. The salt chunks went through his jeans and underwear, and buried deep beneath his skin, like it was all part of some sadistic curing method. He made it home on his own but had to go to Emergency after that, so they could fish out the salt. He wore a bandage and couldn't sit for a month.

The goal is to get to the house. Kaleb Whitby made it the closest, right up to Lawson's front door mailbox—his name's on the lips of every kid on our block. Maybe we can make it closer? Maybe everyone is ready to start talking about us. If we can steal a piece of mail, we're gold. Especially with old man Lawson's name and address printed right there for everyone to see.

"Are we getting Sherry?" asks Peters.

"Shh. Shut up. Keep your voice down," I say. "My mom'll crap her pants if she finds out we're going to Sherry's."

"The record thing?"

"Yep. And now it's a record *and* a lighter thing. So keep it down."

"Okay. Sorry."

"Peters, what's with the skateboard?"

"I have a mom, too, remember? She told me to take it."

Peters's mom's a psychic. No kidding: her signs are pitched at every four-way stop in the neighbourhood. *Jane Peters—Psychic. Palm Tarot Cards Crystal Ball Readings. Helps All Problems*. Each sign has a painted hand with an eye in the middle. Peters did all the artwork. She made the career change from being unemployed after she predicted the death of her sister, who died after a long battle with a terminal illness. Turns out the odds were in Jane's favour. Besides, she never told us about any of the predictions she got wrong.

Peters points his skateboard towards Sherry's place, hops on, and skids across some rocks in the driveway. We stop at the edge of Sherry's yard. The white vinyl siding on their rancher hangs loose, revealing red and blue Tyvek house wrap. Ditches filled with muddy water enclose the yard on two sides, and a narrow plank crosses the ditch that runs the length of the back yard. The only thing missing is a pirate prodding me with a cutlass.

Their yard is a living museum. Animals, at the start of their parade route, emerge from the crawl space under the house. Two cats, just waking, fully extend their hind legs in long sleepy strides. A litter of five kittens, each with a new pair of eyes barely open, pursue Buck (their dog) like paparazzi chasing a film star. The grass grows long and twisted, curling itself into matted clumps of green and brown that easily choke the lawn mower. The yard's filled with cobbled metal and wood structures: four dismantled rototillers, a dozen or so bike frames and bald tires, half a red Radio Flyer wagon decorated with rust blossoms, and three piles of nailed boards. All relics from some glorious undertaking, and in them I see last summer and the summer before.

Ricky, Sherry's older brother, is the master craftsman. He calls the shots and builds everything. Our *Field of Dreams*. We have an idea, and Ricky makes it happen. He borrows from people's yards, goes scavenging at construction sites—whatever it takes. We never ask where he gets the stuff. We know better. One summer, we wanted to make a zip line out of clothesline cable with a 2x10 plank for a seat. *Shazam!* He made it happen. I climbed the cedar to the forty-foot mark, where we had fastened one end of the blue clothesline. The other was attached to a small birch tree eighty feet away; a nice easy trip from tree to tree. *Yeah right.* Halfway across on the maiden voyage, the cable snapped, and I dropped like a flightless bird. I hit the ground, my teeth gnashed; I tasted blood and later lost a filling. I also split the 2x10 plank in two. So I know how Kaleb Whitby felt and so does my ass.

Ricky, in a wash-faded denim jacket and Big Blue jeans with the leg cuffs rolled to narrow bands, nods at me like a construction site foreman when I enter the yard. His jeans cover Daytons fitted with steel toes and tractor treads. Black oil smears, like slug trails, wind their way down his pant legs. Loud music rattles the aluminum walls of his work shed and Brian Johnson with a voice like a gravel truck, telling us how he's back in black and let loose from the noose that's kept him hanging around.

Ricky oozes cool. His chopper, propped against the wall of the shed, is made from fastening long pipes to the front forks of a Factory Kuwahara—probably stolen, probably with the serial numbers sanded off. The entire pedal bike is primered. We watched him beat a kid who made fun of it. "Looks like you got that one off the rez—Black." Wild-eyed, he stomped the kid's head repeatedly outside Mac's Milk, as the Slurpee-fisted crowd, always hungry for someone else's fight, gathered round and chanted, "Fight! Fight!" Ricky's sister had to peel him off.

Back at the work shed, I'm the centre of Ricky's attention and don't know where to stand.

"You got a girlfriend yet, Jeremy?" Ricky asks.

"Still working on that one."

"Jesus, when are you gonna get laid? You gotta be, what, fourteen by now?"

My face is hot. I look at my feet. I'm not sure why every time I come over my lack of sexual experience takes centre stage and I leave convinced every fourteen-year-old has sex hourly on demand, and I'm some kind of weirdo.

"You know, you wait too long, and you'll miss the window, and then you really are screwed. If you don't get laid by fourteen, you never will. Not because you don't want to, but because your dick needs to be used by fourteen or it dies. They call it shelf life. It shrivels, dies and falls off."

Shelf life? Shrivels? Dies? Falls off? I don't have any idea what to do with a girl, and Ricky's the last guy I'd ask. Especially after French-kissing his sister Sherry for twenty-three minutes and putting my hands down the back of her pants last Saturday at Unwin Park. After I wedged both hands in, which took some manoeuvring, I wasn't sure what to do next. And the only reason I put my hands down the back of her pants in the first place? Becky Stone. She prompted me with handwritten notes.

You see, Becky stood a few feet away and watched while Sherry and I made out. Every few minutes, Becky tapped my shoulder and held up a piece of foolscap inscribed with thick purple marker.

Close eyes more! Look like cast member Ret. Living Dead. Time 3 min 12 sec.

She likes tongue IN mouth. Time 7 min flat.

And then she upped the ante.

Put both hands IN her pants. Time 9 min 23 sec.

Now, I know Sherry didn't say a word for obvious reasons, her tongue was busy, but I felt I had to do what Becky said. I don't understand girls, but I understand they're in control, and I don't mind as long as I can kiss Sherry. When Sherry loosened the top button of her pants, I slid both hands down the back. Was I supposed to put them in the front? The back made more sense—

more ergonomic. My fingertips never new such pleasure, bunching the cotton underwear to touch her skin. Her breathing, our tongues entangled like dueling eggbeaters, and the push of her body into mine: this was a foreign, tropical island. I prayed Becky didn't leave; how the hell would I know what to do next? So me and my tongue stayed right there until we reached *13 min and 37 sec.*

"Hey, Jer," Sherry asks me now. "When'd you get here?"

Her black hair—thick and curly—bounces as she walks. With one finger, she hooks a ringlet over her ear. She looks right at me. She's this little bird—oblivious to its beauty—that you could cup in your hands. My breathing quickens. My face is red.

Ricky grabs my shoulder.

"I know what you guys are up to," he says.

I think I'm dead. Does he know about me and Sherry? I imagine his boot tread up close, like a waffle iron stamping the Dayton logo on my face. But he does nothing.

"You're going to Lawson's, right? Be careful. He's a mean son of a bitch."

"Oh, yeah, thanks. We will."

We enter the trail, and I exhale through pursed lips. The sky is bright but still cloud-filled, no sun to be had. Everything has a hyper light quality that makes you squint wherever you look.

We get to the edge of Lawson's wheatfield—the edge of something about to change. I comb the area. I notice the barn door's wide open, and the sugary smell of silage hangs in the air. Attached to the right side of the barn is a fully enclosed chicken coop, but I see no animals; everything's empty, probably clearing it out before the move. In the distance, a storm cloud broils across the sky.

Sherry asks, "Who's going to the front door?"

"I'll go," I say.

"If we get caught, my mom's gonna kill me," Peters says.

"I want a smoke," Sherry says.

"A smoke? Seriously? Now? Look, we can only do this if we work together. No one's going to get caught as long as we take our time. Come on."

We run to the corner of the barn. I look around it, and my heart stops. Lawson is standing twenty feet away.

"Shit. He's right there."

My heartbeat and breathing pick up. We press against the barn, out of view. The summer sun on the barn boards makes them hot to lean on. My feet tingle. I need to piss. I inch back over to the corner. This time Lawson is walking toward the house and away from us. I exhale. He could be a railway conductor inspecting the boxcars in his blue and white striped coveralls. He's old and bald, but big—real big. I motion for Peters and Sherry to stay put.

"It's okay," I whisper. "He's walking toward the house."

Now what? We're just sitting here exposed and begging to get shot by Crazy Man Lawson. *Stupid, stupid idea to come here.* I look around the corner again and now he's heading straight for us. We need to hide.

"He's coming this way!" I hiss. "Get in the chicken coop. Now!"

"The what?" Peters says.

"The coop," I say as I hustle past.

On my hands and knees, I crawl up the plank and plunge into the narrow opening. It slows me, so I wiggle through, Sherry's in next. But Peters gets stuck halfway.

"What now, what now?" Peters asks, his cheeks puffing out and in.

"Grab his arm and I'll grab the other. Pull," I say to Sherry.

"C'mon, Peters, c'mon," Sherry pleads.

Sherry and I pull. Peters inches inside. Crawling together, we go further into the dark. From inside, I look out a knothole. No sign of Lawson. Surrounded by straw, we lean against the interior wall; sitting with legs splayed, catching our breath. We're safe. Strips of light coming through gaps in the siding catch the floating dust motes. The real chickens are gone, so we can stay here forever.

Sherry, a slight flutter in her hands, pulls out a brand-new pack of Export As. It's a green package, with a Highland dancer in the corner. I watch her in this forbidden ritual. Sherry's our beautiful dancer, placing her hands lightly here and then there. With that same grace in each slender finger, she unwinds the plastic wrapper and lets it fall. Pushing her thumbs into the bottom of the pack, the top pokes out like a desk drawer. She tugs the foil. There they are—twenty-five little beauties. She reaches in her back pocket for my mom's lighter. I gave it to her last Saturday after we kissed.

"This is a *baaad* idea," Peters says, using his skateboard for a seat.

"Oh, you want one?" Sherry asks. "Lemme light this."

Sherry tucks the filter between her lips—the paper sticky with saliva—and it hangs there, a coat on a hook. She slides her thumb across the spark wheel twice and positions the cigarette at the heart of the flame. With her inhale an orange ember emerges, lighting her face from below, and we hear a faint crackle of burning tobacco. She blows sweet smoke into the air. Sherry looks solemn in the hazy half-light. She's about to tell a freaky ghost story. The lighter—on its way to Peters—is fumbled and drops, so Peters moves to catch it but bumps Sherry's elbow. Knocked free, her cigarette's golden ember disappears into straw.

Inside the coop the hay is tinder, and within moments a wisp of smoke appears and searches for a way out but finds none, so it widens into a band until smoke is everywhere, filling all the space between us.

"Get out now!" I yell. "Out!"

Peters goes first. He's stuck again. We lean on him with our shoulders and dig in. The fat bastard's gonna kill us. My eyes burn. I cough.

"Suck it in Peters. Jesus!"

Peters pops out and onto the mud with his skateboard next to him—upside down, wheels spinning. Burning wood crackles, it's the sound of corn in a jiffy pop. One after another, Sherry and I bust out. We turn to watch the flames grow, covering the barn, licking in and out between roof beams. A steady roar and a wall of heat engulf us.

Sherry spins me round and we run for the road out front, our faces smudged. The street's quiet, no neighbours for miles. Neighbours or not, we stand out like kids riding bikes with no hands—against traffic.

"Walk, walk, don't run anymore," I say. "We'll go to the Big Hill."

WEEUWEEUWEEUWEEU. Two neon green fire trucks head straight for Lawson's. I turn to watch. The men on the ladder truck stand in an open bay behind the cab, and there's a flurry of action as they scramble into jackets, helmets, and oxygen tanks. We're all running out of air. I look at Sherry.

"Stop!"

"What?" Sherry asks.

"Where's Peters?"

"I don't know. He was behind me a minute ago."

We stop in a thicket, dark spongy soil beneath our feet. Beads of sweat slide down my face and drip from my chin as I look back from where we came. I tilt my head and lift my arm to wipe the sweat with my T-shirt. We're far enough away, but the burn feels closer: it's bigger, brighter, and sending a black ribbon of smoke up into the sky. I see Peters sprint toward us, panting.

"Hey, dinkus, look what I jacked," he says, waving a piece of Lawson's mail. He places his hands on his knees, waiting for his breath to catch up.

"You're crazy. Did you see Lawson?" I ask.

"Of course not."

What if Lawson's trapped in that barn with flames leaping all over him? He didn't do anything to deserve that, to burn like that—did he? It's going too fast. We need to get home, away from the sirens, the smoke, and flame.

A sharp pain bites my scalp. Nails buried deep, fingers squeeze a fistful of my hair, and I'm wrenched to the ground.

"You little pricks. You thought you were gonna get away with it. Now I've got you right here. And you," he says looking at Peters, "you left your skateboard behind—dumbass!" Lawson shakes the board high with his free hand.

Lawson is defensive-line big, with a meaty face and a knotted grip my fingers can't budge. Peters and Sherry are sideways to me now. Lawson's knee, like a motionless drill bit, presses down on my head. Crunchy soil grit jams my teeth.

Sherry's hand is on Lawson's shoulder, and I can feel it too, like she's touching me.

"Look, Mr. Lawson, it's my fault. I lit a cigarette and it fell. It was an accident. A dumb mistake. Can you let him up?"

Lawson doesn't move.

"If my barn's gonna burn, then you fuckers are burning, too," he says. "These boys are staying put," he looks at Sherry, "while you go fetch that cop over there." He nods at a blue and white RCMP car in his driveway. "I bet they're gonna wanna know why you were runnin'."

Lawson releases my hair, sliding his hand to my neck, and driving my face further into the dark soil.

"C'mon, mister, you're hurting him. Look, you're hurting him. Here... here's your mail back, just take it." Peters says.

Peters lets go of the mail. It swings back and forth through the air like a lazy fallen leaf. Lawson doesn't bite. And in his grip, I feel fear and anger. He's the one scared shitless.

"Get off him," says Peters. "Please!"

Lawson won't let up. I can hear that pitch in Peter's voice. A voice he uses when the tears have stopped and he's ready to fight. He must have run full steam into Lawson. I don't feel his weight. I hear the skateboard strike Lawson's head, like a meat hook into a side of beef.

With a constant buzz in my ear, I drift away on a bed of air. I want Elvis back for an encore, just one more song. I pinch the record firmly between my thumb and forefinger; and hold it so a streetlight flashes the black vinyl. *I'll love you forever, Lizard*, written on the label in Dad's shaky high-school scrawl. While rolling my wrist back and forth, I imagine launching the record like a Chinese throwing star, hoping it will somehow get to Dad. Love airmail: weaving over branches and between tree trunks, it's a super charged Wham-O Frisbee with eyes. But the record slams a tree and shatters. Everything eventually disappears somewhere in the dark.

But that magic 45, that nostalgic relic that Mom can't live without, is nowhere near my dad, it's tucked neatly into a Ziploc bag, hidden above our hot water tank. Push up the attic hatch and you'll see it; nestled between a joist and some pink insulation. And I know that record is just a *goddamn* thing, about a *goddamn* pair of blue suede shoes, and my old man's The King. But I'm ready to give it back. I'm not helping her any by keeping it, and she doesn't deserve that.

With Lawson's weight gone, I roll onto my back, but the rain falls, light at first, then in steady sheets, pelting my skin. I can't see it, but feel its warmth, like a dog's wet tongue licking me to life. Blurry faces emerge to hover, voices droning—,"get up, let's get outta here!" Then it all comes back, and I want even more rain to fall, a deluge: rain so heavy it washes everything away. The soot, the soil, the skateboard, the cops and us—all of it right into life's giant drain. But the rain only tapers, leaving us behind. Peters, Sherry, and I run hard for home, just ahead of Lawson's reach and the blood threading from his chin. Before I round the corner, I look back at Lawson, dizzy and staggering, lost among the trees.

STARTING PEOPLE

"I CAN'T WAIT," Andy says. "But I'm nervous. They sent us a picture of the mother. I want a shot of our pup. And a Polaroid? I didn't know they still made 'em."

Andy sticks the photo back on the fridge, moves to a stool, sits and taps her laptop awake. Gleneyrie Kennels. *A dog is for life.* She scrolls the photos. They're all German Shorthaired Pointers. In her favourite photo, two puppies run through a narrow stream, while a third sits back on his haunches, looking right into the camera. Sunlight colours the splash, maximizing the moment. Andy touches the screen image of the dog, trying to push it to life. She imagines what it would be like to care for that dog. To walk it and have people stare at the dog instead of her.

"Hey, Andy, I read something online the other day and apparently Polaroids are making a comeback," Connor says. He's tall and brooding with thick eyebrows and thin lips. His T-shirt has a hole above the left shoulder where the cat once plucked. He wears khaki chinos and a pair of grass-stained running shoes, the heel counters worn from being slid on and off. He opens the dishwasher, pulls a dirty mug, rinses it, and pours a coffee. He does it all with a slice of toast stuck in his mouth.

"What did you say?" Andy asks.

Connor pulls the toast free, brushing crumbs from his chest. "Polaroids... Polaroids. Wal-Mart sells the cameras, so they must be making a comeback. You know, Wal-Mart—the land of the lost. I swear to God. I was there yesterday. You know that glass bus shelter out front?"

"Yep." Andy's winding the elastic tighter on her pony-tail.

"Well, there's a picnic table beside it and there's this lady changing her kid's diaper. Her cigarette bobbing up and down while she talks into a cellphone and there's an Egg McMuffin, hash brown, and a handful of change piled next to the baby. I swear to God, that's multi-tasking. It was like she was narrating a cooking show or something. She just needed a headset microphone and one of those giant table mirrors. 'Okay, now lift those feet up high so that baby's ass is right off the table. Follow me here, this could get messy, with the baby still suspended place a fresh diaper down like you're laying an extra place mat at the table—'"

"Damn it! Stop talking about babies. You do this every time, every conversation turns to babies. Poof. Right out of a magic hat. How do you think it makes me feel?"

"Right, right, sorry, I do that. I just thought it was a funny little scene."

"Well, it just stirs it all up for me."

"Look, I'm sorry."

"My pregnancy was so easy for everyone else. It's me. My body. My sacrifice. Prenatal vitamins. Eat well. Stop drinking. Morning sickness. No coffee. Monthly check-up. Vaginal exam. Blood tests. Morning sickness. Then, for kicks, lets fuck it all up so I have to start over. Am I getting this right? I did it all."

Connor walks over to where she is sitting and places a hand on hers. Together they are soft and warm. Over the winter they lost their second baby. This one at nine months: fingers and toes, arms and legs, teeth; who knows maybe even a little smile under there; it was moving from one stage to the next, or so it seemed. Bobbing in the amniotic fluid, drinking it, breathing it all in. Its room painted yellow (they wanted it to be a surprise) with a stencil of three frogs—one jumping to a new lily pad. There's a change table, diaper genie, nightlight, and baby gate at the top of the stairs. A small plaque on the wall: *Babies are Such a Nice Way to Start People.*

They had named it Twinkle. Boy, was it active. Some nights they watched it wander across her belly, a trapeze artist below the circus tent. The OB/GYN said it, "Listen guys, you know most miscarriages happen within the first 12 weeks, you've been through that, but this is now, so stop worrying and enjoy this pregnancy."

They left his office, parked in the pregnancy stall at Babies "R" Us and went on a baby binge. They loaded up on onesies, and soothers (the kind you can clip-on), and plastic bowls (covered in cartoon giraffes and elephants), and spoons (with hearts in the handles). After that, they went home and baby-proofed everything: removed the cleaning products from under the sink, capped the electrical outlets, padded the coffee table corners, and strapped the cupboard doors shut. But Andy and Connor didn't know how to cushion the sharp edge of loss. Who does? No bestseller on that one: *What to Expect When You Miscarry*.

What's worse—it feels like everyone knows, even the people you don't want to know. It's life's window jammed open; no curtain, no blinds, nothing between you and the outside getting in. When it came up, they had to explain, wade through the details. What caused it? What stopped the beat? The flow? Did you do something wrong?

"I better get that car ready if you and I want to leave on time for the dog kennel." Connor lifts the car key from the back door hook before going outside.

Andy gets up from the table to watch Connor from the living room window. He approaches the car in time with Maureen Jensen, a neighbour who walks her dog past the house twice a day, every day (she's retired). Maureen's this drone constantly buzzing in the distance, only moving closer when she wants more. Andy and Connor hate her questions, her probing. Connor stands there, his lips no longer move, his eyes stick to the ground and burn a hole in the asphalt. Maureen drops the leash and lifts her arms. Connor steps back, arms down, but Maureen ignores that. She moves in, personal space gone, and gets a hold of him for the one-sided-shit-hug, pinning his arms in the squeeze. She even pats his back like he scored his first goal in soccer. Her dog barks, startling Connor. He thinks he stepped on it.

"Connor, I can't get my head around it. I was walking right here when you two left for the hospital that day. My god, I was standing right here," Maureen says.

Andy and Connor want to replace the bad memories, to stamp them out and colour in something new, something good. Today they will drive to the mainland to see their new puppy. They've already named her Lily. With the neighbour gone, Andy walks out the front of the house, slips into the car and closes the passenger door. *Thunk*. They drive the Old Island Highway, a slow two-laner that runs beside the sea. Andy stares at the beached grey boulders that slip and clank with the waves. She lowers her window, lets in the salty vapour and the sound of screeching gulls.

From the car Andy combs the shore for Japanese tsunami debris, the pieces of someone else's life. The wreckage washes up on beaches further north. Last spring a Japanese registered Harley Davidson landed in the Haida Gwaii. The carrying container broke apart from the wave action, leaving the bike buried half deep in the sand. Andy wonders if it belonged to a Japanese biker. Probably not, but she imagines the owner searching for it anyway—he's quieter, less menacing on foot.

"Can you please stop at Pharmasave? I want to pick up an ovulation kit."

Connor lifts his hand for the fist bump, but Andy leaves hers in her lap.

After Pharmasave they arrive at the Ferry, stop at the ticket booth, pay and park, waiting to board. Connor is off to Starbucks, Andy the washroom. Hundreds of people surround them, but they only notice the babies: being pushed, pulled and lifted, riding on hips and shoulders, carried in Baby Bjorns, being carted around in fully loaded monster strollers with mag wheels, front and rear shocks, and coffee cup holders. Each one of the babies is built for this life too. They are ideal—cute and cuddly, with fresh smiles and wide eyes. Seeing them all, Connor isn't sure if they should add one more.

Connor returns to the car. "One gingerbread Latte for you, ma'am."

"Are we crazy tryin' for another kid?"

"Maybe a little, especially you."

"C'mon, join me in adult conversation."

"Well, everyone keeps saying that having a child changes everything. I think it already has, and we haven't even had one yet. But it's simple. I want it. You want it. And knowing that makes me want it even more."

"I just feel this pressure to do what's next, in spite of it all."

"What do you mean?"

"Find a job, get married, buy a house, and then our parents with their, 'keep trying, don't give up. Have that baby. We want grandkids.' The plan, follow the plan."

"You make it seem like it's all coming from the outside in. I think it's the other way round. It's coming from us. We choose. Our plan."

"Maybe it's coming from all sides. We're surrounded."

A voice from the loudspeaker interrupts their conversation. "The Queen of New Westminster is now loading. Please return to your cars and prepare to board."

Connor starts the engine, drives the ramp up to the ship, and looks down through the railings to watch the ocean's power rise and recede against the granite riprap. The tops of the pilings are slathered in creosote, the bottoms submerged and pasted with barnacles and bright purple starfish—all climbing over one another.

A woman controls everyone's passage onto the ferry. She wears a bright vest and waves an orange baton. She stares drivers down, lifts a free hand and wiggles her fingers, nudging the cars closer and closer. "Okay, that's good, good, stop." Taking each one on, handling it, then setting it in its place. This is how she fills each lane, an architect in the mechanical mating of metal.

Loaded with three hundred cars, the ferry carves its way across the cold green Pacific from Nanaimo to Tsawwassen. Connor and Andy are parked in a shadowy space near the portside hull, below long metal I-beams. There is no car ahead. They'll be first off at the terminal.

"Yes ma'am, front row seats!"

Connor cracks the glove box and reaches for his wallet and phone. Andy closes it. *Click*. She grabs his hand, places it on her knee, and slides it up the inside of her leg.

His fingers dimple her inner thigh.

"I'm ovulating."

"I'm Connor."

She smiles. "Listen, I'm ready to do this again."

"Wait a sec. Here? In the car?" His finger points down, wrist bent.

"I don't care if we're on a satellite orbiting the moon."

She pulls a lever and rolls the seat back. *Clunk*. Reclines. She raises her eyebrows three times—quick. *Show time*.

"There's no one around. Get over to my side."

"What about him?" Connor nods at a Ferry worker placing chocks under the front wheel of a car in the next lane.

"When he goes. Okay?"

"Okay. When he goes."

The worker is up the stairs in the centre of the ship. Andy slides her navy tube skirt up and over her hips. Her underwear goes down, catching a clasp on her sandal, so she wiggle-kicks it off. She's supine. Connor takes off his shoes and loosens his belt, but he can't get it all done under the steering wheel. He pulls only one pant leg off, leaving the other bundled around his ankle.

Connor laughs, "It's Friday night and we're in the high school parking lot. Keep a look out for your dad's red Camry. Wait a minute; this is sex at sea level. Is that a club? Must be a club. Should I film this? W-W-W-dot-fifty-shades-of-ferry."

"Connor. Jesus. Focus. And stop talking. Please."

Stepping over the console, he positions one foot between hers on the passenger side, like he's stepping into cold water.

"Watch my coffee. It's hot."

He readjusts his planted foot for balance and drops a hand on the headrest, but he catches some of Andy's hair. "For fuck's sake." He steps his other leg over, but his belt swings loose, the buckle, like a wrecking ball, strikes Andy's knee. *Whack*. "Ouch! Jesus! What the hell?"

"Oops. Sorry. Sorry."

He's prone. She grabs hold of him. No kiss; their lips don't touch. *Focus... Connor... focus.* But the rhythmic squeak from the car seat keeps getting in the way. He needs to concentrate—but that sound. His left heel gets stuck in the cave below the glove box. He stops to pull it free and start again. He looks at her. He closes his eyes. He hears the speed of her breathing and her soft moans. He feels the build. She presses her nails into his wrists. His legs shudder. Both arms buckle and he flops onto her. A strand of phlegm strings his open mouth, stretching in and out as he breathes.

She pulls Connor tight and bites his ear. They stay pressed together, his sweat absorbing into her cotton dress. The window's thick with steam. She slides her tongue over his cheek and presses her lips to his. After the kiss, Connor goes back to his seat.

Andy walks her feet up the glove box and across the windshield, leaving small footprints behind. She inches her toes closer to the seam of the roof. She's a gymnast in the Pike position, wedging her hands below her hips to hold the pose.

"Do your thing boys. Swim. Swim. Swim."

Connor feels like a city worker—his job is done. He's sitting there trying to look busy. He just needs a shovel handle propped under his chin. So he dresses.

"Well, I'm going into the light for something to eat."

"Can you bring me back a burger? Please."

Two hours later the ship lurches as they touch the Tsawwassen dock. The cars unload. *Clunk-clunk, clunk-clunk, clunk-clunk*. They drive Highway 99 and spot a police car hidden below an onramp, gunning for speeders on the flats near Mud Bay. Andy and Connor arrive at a subdivision of brand-new homes. *Welcome to Serpentine Crescent.* They follow the black ribbon of fresh asphalt through the entrance.

"This is not it."

"Supposed to be. Look," he shows her the text, "34 Still Water Road."

"Ya, but Connor you saw the photos on the kennel's website."

All of these houses are built on top of one another and scattered below a string of power lines; a series of giant lattice towers that carry the electricity up and over a neighbouring hill. The buzz and hum make permanent background noise. The tiny yards are incomplete—no lawn, no beautiful flowers, no trees—just scraped earth with wiry roots poking the air. The homes are packed tight, like dinner rolls in a baking pan.

"This is weird. Where's the farm? The dogs? Eight full-grown dogs? Plus puppies? Maybe we should call?"

Connor calls.

He talks to Janice, she's the owner, but he's confused. He hears dogs barking through the phone.

"You're at the right place, just walk around back."

They walk to the back and see the farmhouse pictured on the website (Janice's sister owns the new build). But it looks like the entire farmhouse was dipped into a bucket of bleach and left until the colour ran out. Several round boulders lie on the grass, having fallen from the walls of the home, now pockmarked, like someone attacked it with an ice cream scoop. Entire sections of roof shingles are missing, and the porch is a rotted wood frame.

Janice approaches Andy and Connor. She has tangled hair with grey roots—the ends dyed red. Her hair is an afterthought, like someone dropped it on her head before she stepped out the front door, hoping to add a thoughtful touch, like a colourful scarf, sunglasses or a hat. But it's not. She wears a bright yellow woolen shawl covered in dog hair and twigs.

"Hello, nice to finally meet you both."

She shakes their hands and motions for them to follow.

They walk the buckled sidewalk to the front door of the farmhouse. Janice opens the door by leaning in with a firm push. A musty odour, like wet towels left in the wash for days, mixed with feces and urine ploughs their noses. This is the dog's house. The carpet is torn. The floorboards exposed. There are chalky holes in the Gyproc, scratch marks down the doors and walls, and chunks of moulding lie broken, chewed, and splintered. Janice walks ahead down the hall. Andy looks at Connor, leans forward, and opens her palms, while mouthing, "*What the fuck?*"

Janice stops in the kitchen and sits at the table.

"We've had problems with squatters on our property. So I moved in. It's been a rough winter for me, ya know. I lost my job in November and then this pain in my lower back started up. I'm on disability now. Do you guys want something? A cup of coffee?"

"No," says Connor, "We're good. Thanks. We're really just looking forward to seeing the puppy."

"I'm not sure if I should show her to you guys."

The lines in Andy's face grow deep, magnifying her frown. One eyebrow arches.

"Listen, Janice, we came all this way. Two hours on the ferry. Three hours of driving. We want to see the dog. We need to see her before we make the purchase. You knew this," says Andy.

"Oh, I know, I know. It's just that your pup... well you shouldn't really see her like this, that's all. You're not going to like it. But okay, okay. I'll get her out. C'mon."

They walk outside to a stand-alone garage with a metal roll-up door. Connor and Andy hear the dogs locked inside. Janice stabs the key into the silver handle and twists. This sets off an explosion of barking. The dogs hammer at the door. Janice lifts it. Andy and Connor step back. Dogs funnel out, turning and sniffing whatever they get their wet noses on—a shoe, a leg, some fingers. Their stubby tails twitch like upright pendulums. Andy and Connor bend to pet as many as they can, before they scatter across the front yard.

Lily is there, with two other pups. It is clear why Janice does not want to show her; there's a golf ball-sized cyst on the crown of her forehead.

"Awe." Andy picks her up. "What's wrong, buddy? What happened to you, huh?"

The mother is at Andy's feet with a low growl. Her lips curl, showing teeth.

"Careful," Janice says. "Better put her down."

Andy does.

"What happened?"

"She had a cut and then an infection. Don't worry it'll heal in no time."

"Have you taken her to the vet?"

"Ya, but you know they just want your money. I'm not pumping my dogs full of chemicals. Besides, this will take care of itself."

The mother's fur is the colour of rust and she is slightly smaller than the other dogs. She circles, sniffing and licking Lily's face. A different pup from her litter comes close, nuzzling her side. The mother growls, turns, and nips the pup on the backside. It squeals and runs off. The mother has a small plumb-coloured scab above her front knee that is surrounded by a tan border of dried mud. The big dogs pass, stepping onto and over the pups. The mother jerks her head to watch.

Andy pulls Connor close.

"Connor let's take her, get her treated ourselves and bring her home."

"It's not that easy, Andy. She needs to be weaned. Remember? She has to eat solid food on her own. She's not ready. We can't just—"

"I don't give a shit! That dog's not staying here tonight."

Connor pinches the skin on the bridge of his nose and exhales.

"Janice," Connor says. "We want the dog. We'll take her home today if that's okay?"

"I don't know. She is not eating on her own yet and I'd prefer if you waited till her head clears up."

Andy remembers her second pregnancy. After nine months there were no signs—zero. Sure, there was some blood that morning, but that was normal; the baby was coming. The pain started in her uterus and radiated outward, at its peak it was a car horn on the brain; a blast, so deep and severe—it felt like it would force everything inside, out. She steadied herself on the stair banister, closed her eyes, sucked air in and blew it out through pursed lips, like she practiced in Lamaze class. A flush of warm liquid travelled her leg and drizzled the carpet, and with it, the pain passed. She cradled her beach ball belly with her forearm, rubbing three large circles into it with the fingers from her other hand. *Hold on, Twinkle, hold on.*

Halfway down the stairs she felt dizzy and called Connor. He was in the yard. Her overnight bag was packed. She backed the car down the driveway, honked and waited. He talked her into letting him drive.

At the hospital Andy looked out from birthing room 6A onto a courtyard of blue spruce, the tips of the branches showed a foot of new growth. The view and the big room were theirs; no one in 6B. The nurses joked with Connor, asking if he would be able to work the camera and cut the cord at the same time. A fetal heart rate monitor filled the room with assurance on every baby beat. But their source of joy and anticipation ended when the baby slid out stillborn, their blood no longer mixing. Alarms, lights and eight new people crowded the room wearing blue caps, surgical masks and rubber gloves. With their faces hidden, Andy strained to hear their voices.

"What? What is it? What's going on?"

No one knew how to respond. No one moved. No one smiled under those masks, or laughed, or did any of the things they were supposed to do when a baby was born. And none of the crying in that room came from their baby girl. Not a sound. Still, the nurse dressed the baby, swaddled her in cotton and gave her back to Andy to hold.

Connor watched. Andy rocked the baby, and massaged her tiny, fisted fingers open with her thumb.

"Maybe they're wrong. Maybe they made a mistake. There's still a chance. Jesus Connor, help me with this."

Connor gives Janice extra money because it's the only way she'll let Lily go. On the drive back to the ferry Andy phones the SPCA and describes the living conditions at the kennel. She hangs up. She looks at Lily in the back seat, shaking on a blanket and unclicks her seat belt, reaches back and slides both hands underneath her, lifting Lily like a warm pie onto her lap. Andy strokes the puppy over and over, until she relaxes and stays where Andy wants her.

"We're gonna love you," she says placing a hand on Connor's shoulder.

TRACE

SOLENNE AND JESSIE sit side by side at the window of It's a Fine Grind, a coffee shop on the King George, glancing up from white phone screens, like they're eyeing black flies buzzing their last meal. Words travel from mouth corner to mouth corner, but seldom with help from their eyes. Most of their dialogue is perfunctory, broken, and grammar free—they like it that way. LOL.

"Yep, and then she says, 'I don't want our relationship to be forced,' and that's what I find *soooo* fucking annoying," Jessie says, thumb drumming his screen.

"So'd like, you ask Nicole what she meant by *forced*?"

"Yep. She just stopped texting. Pow! Right there, like she was hit by a tsunami and swept out to sea."

"Did you see the video I sent? This guy is standing on a delivery truck rolling this pallet of bricks onto the liftgate. He moves it close to the edge, but pushes too far, and everything goes right over—catapulting the guy way up into the air. He lands *splat*"—she claps her hands—"right on the concrete about ten feet from the truck. It's hilarious."

"He dies?"

"Well, he rolls around in agony for a while, so probably a broken bone or two."

"Are you sayin' I'm *that* guy?"

"No, no. Maybe we're all *that guy* and life is jerking us all around, tossin' us here and there, every which way, I don't know. Hey, ya think Nicole and her phone might be bobbing around near White Rock?"

They look at his phone like churchgoers at steepled hands, expecting some kind of miracle. And there it is, a pulsing green bull's eye planted on a street map.

"Nope... nope. She' s still at home, Scott Road and 84."

Jessie wants to slide his hand under that green dot and place it right next to him, but he doesn't have an app for that.

"Well, Delta's close to the Fraser, so your tsunami theory could still hold water."

His blue eyes draw, like a receding wave. She looks longer, a second more, hoping something will surface. Jessie's phone goes off, shakes and sizzles like bacon in a pan. A woman, in mid bite, turns to stare; she looks like she's come across a foul odour. The ring tone plays out entirely and they hear Rick Springfield lamenting Jessie's success with women, and wanting to have Jessie's girl.

Solenne looks up and slides a hand down her face. "Oh, God."

Jessie answers. "Hello? No... no. Where did you see the sign? You sure? We took 'em all down. Look, that's great, but we found the dog three weeks ago, so that one, the one you have, is just-not-my-dog. Get it? Yep. Thanks. Bye."

"I bet it's some homeless guy. Picks out a stray, bathes it and phones you—some kinda half-baked plan. A two-thousand-dollar reward for a missing dog?"

"What can I say? She loves the dog more 'n me."

A month ago, Nicole's chihuahua, Hercules, went missing. Nicole let him into the backyard for his morning pee, and then he was gone. Someone forgot to latch the gate. Nicole was hysterical. She phoned Jessie. Repeatedly. They searched every backyard, side street, garage, open field, and wooded area in the neighbourhood. Finally, they had something to work on together. They knocked on doors like a pair of politicians the night before an election. They couldn't find Hercules anywhere. After forty-eight hours, Nicole stopped eating. She stopped sleeping. She stopped everything.

A trip to Minuteman Prints and five hundred copies of *Help us find Hercules—Reward for his safe return—$2000.00* (with colour photo included—his head cocked sideways) rolled out. Jessie knew the reward was crazy high, but there was no talking Nicole down. She learned early that money's a way out. The posters went up on telephone poles and bulletin boards, bus stops, outside the ice rink and the community centre. "How about we put one at the Wave Pool?" They called the SPCA, and they ran a lost dog graphic on the town's electric sign.

With all the reward money, interest in Hercules shot to celebrity status. The thing is Herc was sitting on Nicole's front step wagging his sausage tail fifteen minutes after the last poster went up. But it's Jessie's cell on all the posters, and the calls just keep on comin', day after doggone day. Forget the lottery, Hercules is a real chance at two grand. Now he's everyone's lost dog.

"I still say get rid of your phone, or at least change numbers. C'mon, is it worth the hassle?"

"I'd die without my phone. I'll just ride it out."

"Tell me, why a poster in front of the methadone clinic?"

She starts to cackle, making small fists and leaning her head way back. "Sure, they're taking their methadone—they'll take methadone, Listerine, Pam cooking spray, rubbing alcohol, you name it—as long as it tides them over, 'til they have enough dough for the real deal. Kapow! Two grand for a dog?"

"You sure you're not a motivational speaker. You make me feel like turning my life around."

She smiles and punches his shoulder.

"Ouch. We took all the posters down. What else do you want me to do? Anyway, gotta go, bus comes in fifteen minutes."

"Where to?"

"Nicole's."

"You invited?"

"No."

"She has Herc back. I don't think she needs you anymore."

"What?"

"I don't think she treats you very well." She turns her coffee mug. "That's all."

"How's she supposed to treat me?"

"With some respect. I mean, did she even ask if she could use your number on those posters? Does she ever ask?"

"Whatever. Listen, thanks for the coffee."

Jessie gulps the last of his mocha, corners coffee cake crumbs with his fork and fingers them onto the tines. Solenne slides a knife over, brushes his elbow and whispers, "Neanderthal. The knife. Use the knife."

He does. When he gets up, he makes a mug-plate tower, balancing it on the counter.

Jessie nods at the barista.

"Thanks."

Back at the table, he kisses Solenne on the cheek, and they hug. Solenne picks a cat hair from his sweater, letting it fall.

"Come." Jessie offers. "Walk with me to the bus."

Jessie pushes his arms into his jacket and tucks his phone into his pocket. They leave together in the rain. Up goes his umbrella. Whenever they walk, rain or shine, Solenne rests one hand on his shoulder, even while texting like he's her periscope into the here and now. Then it spills out.

"What am I doing?" Jessie says. "Ya know, I probably spend more time with you than anyone else."

He turns to face her, but Solenne's still texting, and she walks right into him. Her phone slips. She bats it like a Ping-Pong ball from left to right on its way down to the pavement. She cushions the fall with her outstretched boot, snatches the phone up, and wipes the screen back and forth on her shirt, before pocketing it.

"Sorry," Jessie says.

"That was close. Wait, what did you say?"

"You. I was talking about you."

"Well... what about me?"

"I like spending time with you, that's all."

"Me, too."

"Do you ever want more?"

She stares, raising a mouth corner.

"How much more, Romeo?"

He hands her the umbrella. "I'm serious."

"Look, you got this backward. This is not *our* conversation. I mean, it's not the conversation you and I should have. You need to talk to Nicole."

"Why?"

"For starters, it's kinda weird, Jessie, it's kinda fuckin' weird. Don't you think? You have a girlfriend. *Jesus.*"

"Don't get mad."

"You know that is the worst thing to say to someone who is mad, right? Talk to Nicole first, not me, that's all."

"Okay. Alright."

"Look, there's your bus."

Solenne turns, flipping her hood and pulling the drawstring tight; her face encircled by the porthole. Beads of rain run down her jacket. She knows when they shoot an outdoor movie scene, they make everything wet, cover it with water; the sidewalk, the buildings, the ground, the plants. It makes for a better picture, a sharper image. In real life it never works. It rains all the time, but the clarity seldom comes. Solenne looks at Jessie looking at her from the back of the bus, his face resting above the Budget Brake & Muffler ad. He gives a faint wave, smiles and raises both hands. *I give up.* She wants to run after him.

Jessie sits, and something moves inside him, too, but the bus rolls away, everything's in motion. After a few minutes, he sees the White Spot restaurant, stands and presses the yellow strip at the base of the window. *Ding. Ding.*

Maybe his pocket isn't zipped, or maybe the smooth edge got caught up and never made it all the way inside. Whatever the reason, when he removes his jacket and puts it beside him, his cellphone slides out and into the little gap between the seat and the side wall.

Fish is tall and thin. He steps onto the bus wearing a jean jacket swollen from the rain, drops some coins into the fare box, grabs his transfer from the driver and brushes past Jessie, before he steps off the bus through the side door. Fish finds the phone. Looking to see if anyone notices, he picks it up and plops it into his inside pocket, snapping the button closed. He smiles. He tells himself he's lucky that way, just like his mom. She could find a four-leaf clover in any patch of grass. She's dead now. There's a salmon tattoo on his right forearm. Homemade, he did it with ink from a Bic pen, before he went into Willingdon Youth Custody. The tattoo led to an infection, so the dorsal fin's misshapen. He tells people that some fish in real life are like that, too—with a fucked up dorsal fin. Either way, on the surface, that fin's a warning: it marks something below, something monstrous.

He breaks in between 2 and 5 a.m. when people are still home. He eases in through a basement window or slips past a jimmied door. Breathing quiet, moving slow, in, around, and over the furniture. He explores every room in the house and finishes by sitting next to their beds to watch them sleep. Their chests rise, then fall, and there's a whistling when they breathe. Sometimes, he even hears a mumbled word or two from their dreams. And he knows they all have beautiful dreams—the parents about the children, the children about the parents. The nuclear family. The one that could explode at any moment.

But one night Fish sat for too long, and this lady woke up screeching with the religious fervour of someone who was witnessing an act of God—but it was no angel beside her bed. And Fish knew the dark was no place to be with a screaming, hysterical woman. Someone awake. Someone who could see you. But he was too slow. She slid out of bed and onto the floor like a waterspout, her arms flailing in the dark—sucking everything in and beating it back out again. Fish was getting whaled on.

Backpedaling, he tripped over a racoon slipper and landed on a two-foot sculpture from Barbados, bouncing his skull off the sharp edge of a bird basket the carved woman carried on her head. He stood, then tumbled down a set of stairs, *thump, thump, thump,* leaving blood streaks on the banister and walls. He burst through the front entrance, leaving the screen door hanging by a hinge. If you'd watched it all go down, you'd have thought he made it. You'd have thought he got away.

How was he supposed to know the cops had a dog? A German shepherd named Sergeant, and that dog didn't give a rat's ass about the rain, the dark, or blackberry bushes, or clothing, or human flesh, or his dead mom, or all the shit he'd been through in his life. That dog smelled Fish's blood; his scent was in the air. Sergeant buried his canines into Fish's left calf like a fork in Jell-O, and dragged him down, the same as all of those padded Michelin Men in training. Fish was Sergeant's first collar. The police connected Fish to eight B and E's in the neighbourhood—a star was born. Fish got six months, and Sergeant? The front page of the *Surrey Leader*.

Now the cuffs are off, Fish is free, and someone else's cellphone suits him fine, especially when it's just sittin' there, belongin' to no one. It's kinda like finding a chocolate bar on the floor at the grocery store. Off the rack? Mine, all mine.

Jessie knows his phone is gone. He thinks he dropped it on the bus. He does a mental scroll of what's on it: photos, debit card, bus pass. His mouth is dry, and there's a pang of dizziness. *Shit. Shit. Shit.* He calls Solenne on a pay phone. He isn't even sure how many coins to plug in.

She traces it like he asks. The phone shows up in a parking lot beside the Turf Hotel in Bridgeview—the armpit of Surrey.

"Well, don't go alone, okay?" Solenne says. "I'll keep calling the phone. You call the police."

He does. The dispatch asks, “Is the phone stolen or lost and found?”

“How the fuck should I know?”

There is a pause on the line. The dispatch responds, “Look, we’re not sending a car, if that is what you’re after. Remotely wipe the data, then arrange to meet the guy at the police station for an exchange—that’s my best advice.”

Like that’s ever gonna happen. Jessie wants his phone back now. So he’s going to go get it.

At 11:00 a.m., the Turf parking lot’s wide open—almost. There’s a lowered blue Civic with tinted windows parked below the hotel’s neon sign. On the sign, a jockey sits atop a horse galloping along in phi-phenomenal glory. Even the horse and jockey got it right: get the hell outta here!

Jessie steps from the bus to the gravel parking lot. His heart pushes up in his chest. His fingers twitch. He fumbles to get his umbrella up. He stops. He looks at his shoes, closes his eyes and breathes; his diaphragm goes down and in, while his chest goes up and out before it collapses again. He thinks about turning back, about another coffee with Solenne, about how fun the start of something can be. How she likes to kick the soles of his shoes while they walk, so he takes these giant steps. *Check out my moonwalk!* And how they laugh, because he looks like such a dork.

But the phone is right here, just a few regular steps away. For as long as you can feed it, the virtual world buzzes and sparks, showering you in a regular stream of activity and demand. A means to connect with everything.

He stands next to the driver's door. With the window partly down, low, thumping bass, the kind that ripples water in a glass and rattles anything loose, makes the song unrecognizable. He drives a hand into his pocket, leans his head back, turns and walks away from the car.

He hears his phone ring. "That's my fucking phone."

He stops. He goes back, closes his eyes and knuckles the driver's window, *tap, tap, tap,* a real-life touch screen. The music stops, the window drops and out comes the smoke. Jessie steps back.

"Hey," Jessie says. "How's it goin'?"

"What?"

"Maybe you can help me. I'm looking for my phone. I left it on the bus this morning. iPhone. Blue case. You seen it?"

The driver looks up at Jessie with his eyes wide, head nodding, poking his chest with his thumb. "Our help? You want our fucking help? Do we look like the Red Cross?"

The phone goes off again. Jessie glances from driver to back seat. He sees Fish, knees tucked in, eyes closed, head resting on the soft polyester upholstery.

"That's it!"

The car starts. Jessie opens the door and wraps his fingers around the window frame, pressing his palm to the rubber seal. Just when he's about to pull himself inside, the car lurches, jerking his arm. He drops the umbrella he wishes was an anchor. Another quick burst from the front wheel pings gravel off the underside of the car and into his legs. Now Jessie's caught up in it, before he has time to let it all play out in his head. He walks beside the car, stepping faster and faster, like he's starting out on a treadmill. The driver laughs. Jessie's jogging, gripping the door; man against machine. He feels superhuman, like he could lift the car over his head and shake out what's inside. But Fish is awake.

"You little fucker," Fish says. "Let go. I mean it!"

The phone or the car? He can't.

Gunshots, *crack-crack-crack*, break's Jessie's grip, they break everything. He crumples to the gravel, brake lights flash, everything stops dead, except the climbing gun smoke drifts. The driver door's pulled shut. *Thunk.* And that lowered blue Civic jumps onto the King George. Its muffler sparks the asphalt, and the front tires squeal.

THE WISDOM OF NO ESCAPE

WITH A FILET BLADE against her jugular, her mother is pushed the way the inmate wants to go. Like the figurehead on the bow of a pirate ship, she's placid and proud lines carved into the wood. Four guards watch from above, rifles drawn. But in this particular dream, they're props and each guard and gun is a cardboard silhouette that tips and wobbles with the wind. The air blows cold and smells like singed hair. At this point Kate wakes up. Every time.

But last night Kate didn't have the dream.

She's in the bathroom, using her phone's camera to help her reapply her lipstick. There are no mirrors in this church bathroom, so what can't be seen remains hidden. She caps the lipstick and places it in a dry spot on the ledge of the sink. Holding her phone up behind her head, she snaps a picture of her Celtic knot—the braid that took hours to build. According to the stylist, "Nothin' will loosen that sucker," and it looks like he was right. Pinching and spreading her fingers for the zoom, Kate sees everything's locked in place. *Better be. Cost me a bloody fortune.* It's the missing earring that's not right. She pulls her naked lobe, stretching the skin until it whitens, then looks to her shoulder and the tile floor. Finding nothing, she removes the other earring. The earrings her father said she had to wear.

"They'll work," he told her. "It'll mean a lot."

What do you do with your dead mother's stuff? When Kate was young, she secretly dressed in all her clothes—there weren't many—even putting on her old makeup. It brought her closer. The Gunne Sax peasant dresses with the flutter sleeve: four in total, and a pair of tan clam diggers. The shoes Kate loved, the wedge sandals with white laces, and especially the green clunky platforms. She enjoyed the sound they made. *Ka-thunk, ka-thunk, ka-thunk.* Her father did not.

"Never touch her things—ever."

And as Kate got older, he forbade her from talking about her death altogether, especially to strangers. And everyone was a stranger.

"Kate, you must promise," he grabbed her wrist and pulled in time with the words, "to-never-ever-talk-about-it. It hurts *me* when you do. Understood?"

He always used the past tense, as though an agreement was already reached. But it was Kate who had to protect him from the past.

Everything Kate learned about her mother's murder came from the Internet, the government inquiry report, and archived articles in *The Columbian* newspaper. It was her mother's first year as a social worker at the B.C. Penitentiary. She was an advocate for prisoners' rights, and part of a small group who fought the use of solitary confinement.

But it's Kate, on her wedding day, who feels alone.

She smooths her dress and returns everything to her clutch.

Ready to exit, she puts a hand on the door and waits. *Why do I continue to lie?*

"There's the bride," her father says waiting for her outside. "In the middle of something big, and her head's a million miles away."

"I'm ready." She swats his shoulder. "Hard part's over, right?"

"Suppose."

"Where's Lionel?"

It was the three of them at the wedding ceremony—Kate, her father, and Lionel. More of a formality than a celebration. Something small is all Kate wanted.

"Car. I'll be there in a minute."

It's her father's green 1973 Chevy Impala. The long lines of metal create a car so wide it doesn't fit the stall.

Kate gets in the back next to Lionel, her freshly minted husband. His pant legs ride up on his shins, showing the top of his socks, one is navy and the other black. Kate snaps a sock band with her finger.

"Well, who the hell cares," he says brushing her hand away. "The sock is the most useless piece of clothing. Think about it."

"It's going well." She grabs Lionel's hand. "Remember, do not bring up her death, or he'll lose it."

"He has to talk about it at some point."

"Maybe he does, maybe he doesn't. I'm not here to push him—"

"And there he is."

The door squeaks open, and her father gets in the driver's seat.

"All set. You guys ready?"

"Let's rock and roll," Lionel says looking at the back of her father's head. "So, where'd you get it, Mr. McKenna?"

"What?"

"The car," he says, bouncing in the seat and looking around the interior.

"After Ann and I got married." He holds up the key. "She talked me out of a red Barracuda. Insisted on a family car. Dam's Lincoln Mercury on Fraser Highway. Dealership's still open."

"You let her talk you out of one of the original muscle cars? Imagine if you held on to that for forty years. Those are worth real money."

The car rumbles to life, drowning out Lionel's voice.

"If I got this right," her father turns on the radio, "it's out to Bear Creek for a couple pics and then over to the pub?"

"Yep," Kate says, "Castle Pub for two."

"Pub for two—you and Lionel. Not sure I want to go."

The Castle Neighbourhood Grill is built in the gatehouse of the former B.C. Pen. Most of the other buildings are gone.

"I know you're not big on the place." She lowers her window an inch. "But Lionel's mom wanted to do something nice to help celebrate. We'd appreciate if you came. It's decent pub food."

"It's your day Katie bird. I'm there."

"Kate told me you worked at the Pen years ago," Lionel says.

"I did," her father replies, indicating and then changing lanes.

She watches her father's grip tighten on the wheel as they roll along the King George. Traffic is heavy across the three lanes headed north. They make every green light, but her father slows in front of a large rezoning sign and turns off the radio. He lifts a finger from the wheel and points.

"Surrey Drive-in. Remember, Katie? I wonder if people have time for a drive-in these days."

"I remember," she says, sliding her hand along the door panel.

"We took this car."

"Your mother wanted to see *Blue Lagoon* and it was horrible." Her father laughs. "I mean, Brooke Shields couldn't convince anyone of anything, even with a loaded gun. Your mother said a fourteen-year-old girl shouldn't have been cast in that role. So young and stranded on a tropical island. Lord of the Flies it was not. Your mother had a thing for romance." Her father briefly wears a smile. "For true love."

"I wish I could have met her," says Lionel.

"Brooke Shields?" Kate laughs.

"No. Your mom. Kate doesn't talk about her much, what was she like?"

Adjusting the rear-view, her father locks Lionel in his gaze, "Drop it." Directing his eyes back to the road, he speeds up to pass the other cars.

With an unlit smoke scissored between her fingers, Kate motions for Lionel's lighter. He leans back and straightens his leg, digging in his pocket. He holds the lighter up and presses the button, it's like a mini blow-torch. She leans in, her eyes reflecting the small flame.

"I'm worried," Lionel says to Kate. "All that hairspray." He lifts his thumb, extinguishing it.

She rolls her eyes, snatches the lighter, lights up and takes a drag, blowing the smoke out the one-inch window gap.

"It's that dream," Lionel whispers. "Got you riled."

Kate shakes her head and whispers, "Stop," pointing her smoke at her father.

The three of them sit in the car with its long vinyl seats, radio off, and compete for the silence. With all the space in the car, it's as if in the past—in 1973—they wanted to give everyone all the room they needed and more window to watch the world go by. For Kate, each new year means that front seat gets more empty.

Kate picks a piece of rag tobacco from her lip. Flipping up the ashtray lid, she drops it in. "Could've rolled these a little tighter, Lionel."

Kate sees the two metal girders of the Pattullo Bridge rise from the Fraser like a pair of sturdy arms. The river swirls below like cold creamed coffee. Each arch is filled with every angle of crisscrossing metal—all covered in orange paint. Cars move over the bridge deck carrying people in and out of the city, like ants scaling a leaf. People so intertwined they need one another to know freedom and confinement, trust, and betrayal. Where are they going? Can't we lock 'em up? The whole damn lot of 'em? She takes a drag, then taps off a column of ash.

"Cost you a pretty penny," her father says, "to eat at the pub."

"Lionel's mom works the kitchen. Food and drinks on her."

Lionel taps a bottle opener on the passenger headrest. "Who wants beer?" He reaches for the beer box at his feet and fully pops the cardboard flaps, removing an ice pack and lifting a sweaty brown bottle. *Pssht.* He places the cap in his suit pocket.

"For you," he says handing her the beer.

"Oh, watch the suds." He pulls it back and wipes the bottle on his pant leg.

She takes a last drag and flicks her cigarette butt out the window before grabbing the bottle. Lionel opens another and places it between his legs.

"Mr. McKenna? It's not every day your daughter gets married. You want one."

"Agreed, but I'll take mine at the park. Keep 'em low at the intersections. Katie, there's a giant pine at the park you must see. Ever walked barefoot on the needles? It's not what you think."

Bear Creek Park is quiet, with plenty of room for the big old car. They get out and her father says, "That's the one." The mammoth pine stands alone at a bend in the path. They walk towards it and notice the long emerald green branches, tipped with sap-covered cones in clumps of three.

"We stood right there for our photo. The tree was smaller then, but not much. It rained while we took our last couple of pictures. That rainwater, after collecting sap from the tree, dripped onto your mother's dress and me too, I suppose. The smell of the sap, it was like butterscotch," he says, picking up a pinecone from the grass and holding it to his nose, "and I smelled it for the rest of the day and into the evening." He tosses the cone back to the ground. "It's the blood of the tree."

The blue sky darkens with cloud. Staring at the grass, Kate watches the cloud shadows move towards the pine. Her father pulls out a digital camera. "See all those needles under the tree? Slip off your shoes and feel them."

Lionel holds her hand as she slips out of her shoes and steps forward. And standing on those soft needles, Kate knows what her father wants her to feel.

"Ready, one, two, three."

Kate, alone, under the tree. A photo record.

Lionel passes her father a beer. He guzzles down half of it and lets out a soft burp, wiping his lips with the back of his hand.

"Man, that's good and cold. How'd you get it so cold?"

Her father sets his beer on a nearby picnic table.

"Here," Kate says to her father and hands over her phone. "Take some with mine. Lionel, come stand next to me."

Crawling over the white clover blossoms, a bee stings Kate in the gap between her first and second toe, "Jesus!" and she falls to the grass, clutching her foot.

"Get it out!" With her hands shaking, Lionel grabs her foot.

"Here, let me see."

The insect is gone, but the stinger remains, inflaming the skin.

"Just a second, this will help. I got it."

He pinches out the stinger and smears it onto the grass.

"Of all things," Lionel says. "Mr. McKenna can you go back to the car and grab that ice pack from the beer."

"How could something that looks so harmless," Kate says pulling up fistfuls of grass, "sting so much?"

Her father returns with the ice pack.

After a few minutes of applying the ice and waiting, the first raindrops start to fall, big and cold—solo shots fired in warning of the coming downpour.

"It feels better." Kate stands. "And it's not even swelling." She leans her head back to feel the rain on her face.

Her father opens another.

The power steering squeals as they wind their way through the pub parking lot.

"I'll drop you out front and find a spot on the street," her father says. "Either it's parent's night at the Montessori or the pub is giving away free beer."

Sunny Hill Preschool is located above the pub on the second floor of the building.

"How's the foot?"

"Good. Shoe's on. It'll be fine. Glad I'm not wearing flip-flops."

"Man alive, that rain is coming down," Lionel says. "Look at it bounce off the road! We'll have to sit indoors."

Her father drops them at the foot of large cement stairs covered with a red awning. Everything is dripping. Kate wraps herself in a grey sweater and grabs her purse. Getting out she sees her breath and looks through it at the prison walls. They are forty feet high. Kate has never seen them up close. A pair of turrets rise from the entrance, topped with two narrow windows. The Pen is a panopticon design, there is nowhere to hide. Each wall is capped with scalloped edges and painted dark grey. Black wrought iron fencing wraps the patio next to the front entrance. It is cornered by square fence posts with large plastic containers centred on each post and spilling over with pink, purple, and white petunias. The flowers weave through the iron pickets. Half the patio umbrellas are crimson and the other midnight blue and logoed with Sleeman and Granville Island pale ale. The paint, the flowers—all that colour gives the building the look of a child's cardboard cut-out, a White Spot Pirate Pak.

"Hard to imagine this was once a prison," Kate says. "There's a cemetery still, out back, I think they called it Boot Hill. Each grave has an inmate's number chiseled into a brick-sized marker. Those fifty inmates died in there, for just about every reason they die out here. But they had no family to claim their remains."

"Jesus Kate, a little morbid, let's have some fun!" Lionel lets go of her hand and takes the stairs two at a time. "C'mon, you have until midnight and then you turn into a pumpkin!"

Kate limps up behind him.

She swings the double doors and enters to the gentle pluck of guitar strings from "Hotel California."

Kate smells beer, spilled, splashed, and glassed. She reads the sandwich board. *Prison Food Grub: Jail House Burrito, The Slammer Double Burger, and Correctional Cheesecake.* A waitress with two plates heaped with fries and open-faced burgers passes, each patty stacked high with bacon, lettuce, tomato and cheese. Kate's stomach quakes, her mouth waters.

Lionel's mom, Sandra, approaches. "Mrs. Katherine Thomas! How does it feel?" With her arms open wide, she wraps Kate in a hug.

"I'm not used to hearing that yet," she says, resting her chin on Sandra's shoulder.

Sandra steps back. "You look beautiful. Vintage dress?"

"Yes, thanks. It was my mom's."

Kate regrets having brought her up.

"Well, Kate, I wanted to be there, but it was such short notice, I only got the call this morning to let me know your plans."

"I know, we're sorry, it happened quick. But we're together now."

"Come, I have a spot for you two lovebirds away from the kitchen."

She leads Kate by the hand, and they weave through the people. They sit at an empty table at the back of the pub. Lionel approaches with two glasses of beer.

"Where's your tie sweetheart?" Sandra asks him.

"Took it off," he says. "Thing was strangling me."

"Food? You two must be starving. Where's your dad?"

"He'll be here any minute."

"Alright." She taps the menus spread on the table. "What are you going to eat?"

"Park it, Mom," Lionel says. "They already have a waitress, you're off tonight."

"I would love a burger, biggest one they got, but I must go to the washroom first," Kate says, "or I'll burst."

"And your dad?" Sandra asks "Will he eat? Does he want a beer?"

"Not sure about the food, but he'll take a beer even if you put it at the bottom of the ocean. He'll have something dark, like an oil change."

"Guinness then."

With that Kate excuses herself from the table.

The bathroom is dim and empty. There's a condom machine and advertising on the walls. She finds a stall, carefully lifting her dress and bundling it up around her waist, like a lifebuoy. She closes the door and locks it, then hovers above the seat. The relief comes. But someone knocks. Startled she holds her forearm against the door.

"I'm in here."

Her tone, a threat to the listener.

Kate's breathing quickens. She looks below the door, at the shoes—the green clunky platforms, and the hem of the brown Gunne Sax dress. Without moving or breathing she can hear every sound.

"I know," comes the response.

Her mother's voice is unmistakable.

"Lionel seems like a good one. I knew you'd pick a good one. Is it true love?"

Kate fumbles with the latch before sliding it across to free the door. She pushes it hard, slamming the door into the neighbouring stall. There is no one in the bathroom. She steps to the sink, soaps, and washes her hands while staring into the mirror, inhales, and exhales. She turns off the hot and runs the water to get it good and cold, cupping her hands under the stream and splashing her face, indifferent to what little makeup she applied. Ratcheting the lever on the paper towel dispenser she pulls off a handful and wipes her lips and eyes, tossing the paper into the can.

She checks under the stall doors, satisfied there is no one there. She looks at herself in the mirror, and pulls all the pins from the knot, letting her hair fall to her shoulders. She shakes her hair out and rakes her fingers through several times, then tosses the pins in the trash.

In the final confrontation, before the tactical team mistakenly shot and killed Ann McKenna, she bit the inmate's ear clean off and he took a handful of her hair.

Kate leaves the bathroom and walks back to the table.

"You alright?" Sandra asks. "We thought you died in there."

"I'm fine." She sits in the chair next to Lionel. "A bit lightheaded, that's all. I need to eat."

The waitress arrives with a couple beer and two burger plates, setting one of each down in front of Lionel and Kate. Kate takes the ketchup bottle from the table with one hand and a potato wedge with the other and carefully squeezes out a column of ketchup the length of the fry. She pops one end in her mouth, and in between quick bites breathes out the steam, before picking up another fry.

Sandra slides the sleeve of amber beer closer, “It’s for you.”

Kate takes two gulps, sets it down, and wipes her mouth on a napkin.

“We leave for Calgary tomorrow.”

“What’s waitin’ there?” her father asks.

Not looking up from her burger, Kate keeps eating, “About everything I can imagine.”

UNTIL SOMEONE IS NAMED

LOCALS CALL IT The Gale. During the day the white stucco building looks like an Italian villa; at night, a turreted fortress, resting above the valley fog that floats down the Fraser. The Florence Nightingale, its official name, is a private hospital that sits on a hillside in Bolivar Heights. They offer extended care—because there isn't enough to go around.

And tonight, eighty-two-year-old Nora Allen has escaped. Again.

"Checked her room twice," says Maggie, "and the dining hall."

"Main floor bathroom?" asks Joan.

"Empty," Maggie's voice says from a storage room behind the admissions desk. "My shoes, jacket, and car keys are gone."

"She took advantage of shift change and took your car, that's pretty crafty."

"Whose side you on?"

Maggie brushes past Joan and points to her KIA.

"Thank God."

The car alarm goes off, as though her finger point tripped it—headlights flash and the horn blasts in non-stop succession.

"She's pressed the fob! So she's in range. Call Terwott."

Joan whistles low. "She's gonna be pissed."

"Yeah well, it's 11:30, it's dark, and it's raining. Gimme your keys."

"These ones," Joan says, "I lock in the cabinet, so they don't walk off." Joan unhooks them and squeezes them tight.

Maggie rolls her eyes. Joan's such a stickler—following all the steps and checking all the boxes.

"The keys?" Maggie says, holding her flat palm out.

"Hold your horses," Joan says, dropping into a chair behind the computer. "We're here," she drags the cursor across the screen to highlight the top of the missing patient response flow chart, "and you wanna move all the way down here?" She scrolls to *full search of hospital grounds and surrounding neighbourhood*.

"It's her birthday," Maggie says. "I bet she's off to that restaurant, no idea of the time. C'mon, Joanie, the keys. Longer you wait, further she gets." Maggie knows Nora's obsessions. The people she's wronged, the one she left behind, forgotten. And how Nora's guilt has melded with a deep cognitive decline, forgetting names for things like toothbrush or TV remote. "Where is he now?" "Does he have a girlfriend?" were her daily questions. Emotionally undone, a random laugher, with crying fits and a laser focus on all the bad things done. Maggie documented Nora's symptoms in her nightly patient report. Still, Maggie feels responsible for her escapes, because she told her, "Fix it, find him, never too late to do what's right."

"Passenger window doesn't work," Joan says, tossing the keys, a perfect arc into Maggie's hand. "If you roll it down, I can't get it up without taking the door apart."

Rain splatters the entrance window; the wind pushes the doors open and Joan and Maggie look up from the admissions desk after they bang shut.

"Is it a rally?" Joan asks. "You know, one last push? She couldn't even get out of bed yesterday."

"A rally for who—"

"For whom—"

'Fuck, Joan. She doesn't have anyone. Remember her sister, Ada? That look. Like she'd dropped off a sack of clothes at the Goodwill." Maggie knows abandonment—adopted as a child, and placed with a family in B.C.'s interior. She was raised on a mushroom farm. Joking that she was kept in the dark and fed nothing but bullshit. Living on a farm meant hard work and Maggie took that 'drive to get things done' with her into nursing school. The small caseloads at the Gale allowed her to engage with her patients every day and as the years passed, she had come to witness a type of disappearance in all of them. It began with family and friends who stopped visiting, and continued until the end, with patients themselves unable to recognize their own reflection.

Joan knows there's no talking to Maggie when she's like this—it's full-on saviour mode, stand back, get comfortable, and watch the show.

Maggie lifts Joan's jacket from the chair back, "I need this," punching the arm holes, "it's pouring out there."

"You better do something about that car alarm."

"It'll die. Eventually."

Nora craves a Big Mac, large fries, and maybe one of those apple pies, if they still make them. Anything but the powdered mashed potatoes, plopped next to rubbery beef, covered in brown gravy, that they serve at the Gale. She's starving. She looks down at her stolen green Crocs that have MAGS spelled out on the toes in black letter rivets. Gravel embedded in the heel's foam scrapes the asphalt when she walks. *Ksssht... Ksssht... Ksssht.* The sound means Nora's heading somewhere, and so does the pain in her hip. Bone on bone. She stops to rub it, "Get me up that hill." She laughs out breath clouds...they drift up. A muscle spasm straightens her leg and scrunches her face. The laughter stops.

The Vicodin is wearing off. Nora digs into the coat pocket of the yellow rain jacket and finds a stick of double mint, a couple pills, and a bobby pin. She pops the pills, crunching them to powder and swallows them like a food source. "Maggie comes through in a pinch." She unwraps the gum and folds it into her mouth, sucking the winter green to cool her teeth, before she starts chewing. The leg tension fades. She pulls a twenty from the other pocket, rubbing the stiff plastic image of the Queen between her thumb and finger. Daniel, her second son, thought she looked like the Queen. "She's on the $1, $2, and $20," he had boasted to the other kindergarten kids on the first day of school. "What bill's your mom on?"

Rain, lit up below the streetlights, streaks the dark. From where she stands it looks like it only falls under the halo, in that one spot, but it pecks Nora's face. The wet. The rain. Nora has had it all for these eighty-two years and today she starts her eighty-third, outliving her second son, Daniel, and her husband.

Her first son was adopted out the day he was born. She never gave him a name.

Tilting her head, eyes closed, tongue out, she waits, but no drops land. Surrounded by water, Nora's mouth is dry. Pulling the tan scrunchie and releasing her long gray hair, she slips her fingers through the strands, tugging at the knots. *I'm an old woman with old hair.* Gathering it, she replaces the scrunchie, sliding the cool metal bobby pin into her scalp. She shivers. She pulls out Maggie's key fob, points it toward the hospital, and presses the panic button. Twice. *Maybe Maggie can come pick me up?*

She steps over a moss-covered crack in the sidewalk. An old one, filled with thick green fuzz, like a caterpillar. The moss distorts and softens the edges, making it less likely to be fixed. The fracture remains. Nora walks. Slow and steady. She counts and recounts the number of holes in the toes of her crocs. It's thirteen, always thirteen. "One, two, three, four..." There's comfort with each count. *Ksssht... Ksssht... Ksssht.*

When Daniel died three years ago, the need to find her adopted son gnawed away at her.

The Rickshaw's red and blue neon sign flashes down the road: it shows a boy in a sun hat leaning forward, with a wooden shaft under each arm, pulling a woman in a carriage. His sandaled feet flicker, like he's running. The back wheels flash, like they spin. The woman looks out from The Rickshaw. Her red dress encircles her, like a flower pointed in your direction.

"If the sign's on," Nora remembers, "they're open."

Moments of lucidity, the nurse called them, when the memories seep in. And along with them a sense of who Nora is. Where she's been, what she's lost, and who she's loved. A restaurant talk with Daniel remains, alive, in her head. He sits at a table near the entrance as swirls of steam rise from plates of chicken fried rice and bright red sweet and sour pork. The waiter had asked, "Anything else?"

"A Coke," Nora says now, "with lots of ice, and the soy sauce, please?" She leaves the sidewalk, stepping onto the asphalt to cross. She feels the car's headlights climb her face. The car swerves and honks, "Get the fuck off the road, lady!"

"Life's full of surprises. Asshole." Nora continues to a gravel trail on the shoulder.

Her conversation with Daniel returns, "I didn't plan it, you know, I was sixteen—think about that for a sec. Sixteen and in a home for unwed mothers. I was alone. A single bed, a nightstand, an upholstered chair with cigarette burns on a seat cushion where no one ever sat. The furniture was whitewashed. It was like a witness protection program, and my only crime was having a child out of wedlock. It may be hard to believe, but that was a big deal then. Your Aunt Ada dropped off a small suitcase with a broken buckle. My clothes were heaped at the front entrance. She didn't stay to speak, even to ask if I was okay. My family wanted me wiped off the map."

"Mom—"

"You think I caved? Well," she said, picking up her fork and knife. "I fought, fuckin' right, let me tell you. Abortion wasn't legal—I could've gone to jail along with the doctor. What if I quit school, got a job? That place was run by the Salvation Army, and anything done solely for me was considered selfish. Can you imagine? So, they pounded the drum, 'adoption is brave, adoption is selfless, you're in the clear if you have faith in Christ'. The father was gone. No tracking him down. No Internet, no email, no help-me-find-the-father-of-this-child dot com. That army of salvation kept pressing. I was surrounded. I believed them. They would deliver me."

Daniel twirls a fork between his thumb and finger.

"You listening?" Nora asks.

"You're not in front of a classroom anymore, Mom. How many chances did you have to tell it all? Instead, some stranger calls, saying we have a positive match on 23andMe and he thinks he's my brother. I hung up. Can you believe it? I thought it was a scam. After me, he called Aunt Ada because he'd tracked down her name on the release documents. He must have had all the wrong answers because Aunt Ada wouldn't give you up. She refused. Your other son's out there." He pointed at the door with his thumb. "Wandering the dark."

The boy had searched for Nora, his biological mother, for eight years, shifting from wanting to know everything about her to wanting to know nothing at all. When his desire to find her was greatest, he picked a stranger in a crowd, noting her hair colour, height and mannerisms, and manufactured a reunion, a maternal embrace, but he could never create that level of mutual recognition.

After he heard Nora recount her experience, Daniel had shovelled in three spoonfuls of rice, and felt that he was denied something too. Nora remembers the redness around his eyes, the clear liquid running from his nose, and his spoon striking the plate, *clink,* before it hit the floor.

"Don't you wanna talk to him?"

Her eyes glazed over. Her lip corners dropped.

"And say what?"

"Start with, 'You have a younger brother.'"

Daniel stood, stepped on the spoon, and bent the handle. When he left Nora alone at the Rickshaw, a memory returned—the squawk of her first born. His pink skin against her, the warm weight of him, like a cat curling up on your lap. A bundle so tiny and light. His cries mixed with snorts as he rooted for her breast.

She goes on, down the gravel trail. Ahead is a large black dog with tan patches on his shoulders like the highest military rank and thick meaty jowls drawn taut to show teeth. A protector, "this is my path, get your own." Nora stops and looks for an owner, someone to call him off. A yell of, 'Oh he's fine, all bark but no bite.' Instead, this dog's ready for a show down. With the threat comes a flood of fear and disorientation, followed by anger. "Get lost, dog!" She shouts. But the dog lowers his head and takes a wider stance.

Brake lights flash and a car pulls between her and the dog. A young woman winds down her window in a flurry, "Nora, I thought it was you. Looks like you need a ride."

"You got that right, dear."

"Where ya headed?"

"Rickshaw."

"Oh, that's easy enough. I'm going up there for gas."

"I may need a hand getting in."

The young woman gets out and walks to the passenger side and gently grabs Nora under the arms, "That alright?"

"I'm used to being handled."

Helping her in, she closes Nora's door and gets back in the driver seat. The wipers swish.

Even at a distance, in the dark and the rain, Maggie spots her green crocs and the yellow rain jacket getting into the car. "Not bad, Nora," she thinks. "Further than last time." The streetlights whip by, closing the distance between the two cars and between Nora and Maggie.

The young woman adjusts herself in the seat before clicking on the seatbelt.

"Mrs. Allen." She uses the same script every time. "I'm Sarah Diaz—I had you for physics at Len Shepherd." A high school located around the corner from the Gale.

"Anything's possible, but I don't remember much anymore."

Sarah twists the wiper control arm to HI.

"You taught Classical Physics. Reversibility, remember, the idea that theoretically everything runs the same backwards as forwards. The butterfly into the caterpillar and the old man into the child. You're the reason I did physics at UBC."

"Well, dear," she smiles, "you can't blame me for that."

"I can say this... I absolutely hated it. Lasted one semester. I'm a big picture kinda person and I couldn't get there in physics."

She clicks her turn signal, then checks for cars before getting back on the road.

"Aren't we in a system right now?" Nora asks. "A finite one made of fundamental properties that act in predictable ways. How about the car, the road, and the accelerator? Throw in speed, distance, and time and I can tell you with some certainty what will happen. When we will arrive, how fast we will be going, and how much force it would take to stop everything dead in its tracks."

Sarah looks in the rear view, "Well, if that's not tailgating, not sure what is." She pulls into the Rickshaw.

"Here we are."

Sarah is about to get out when Nora places a hand on hers. "Things are added, and things are taken away."

"I'm confused."

"In life, dear."

They pause and Sarah looks down at the wiper control arm, then twists it to intermittent.

Sarah gets out.

When she does, Nora reaches over to lock the doors. *Click.* She slides a leg over the center console. "You can do this," she thinks, "go slow," and grabbing the steering wheel with both hands, brings her other foot over, careful not to bump her head on the rear-view mirror, and drops into the seat.

Sarah pulls the passenger handle, knuckles the window and smiles, "Mrs. Allen?" Muted by the glass. "Looks like you have someplace you really wanna go, eh?"

Nora pokes on the radio and sings along with the Traveling Wilburys, explaining that it's great driving around in the breeze, as long as you live the life you choose. She puts her foot on the brake and slides the shifter into D, when Maggie arrives at the driver's door window, she pounds it with the flat of her hand.

"Don't you dare!" *Thunk, thunk, thunk*. "You've gone far enough!"

"Watch your toes, dear," Nora gently steps on the gas. "I'm off to see the soil I grew up on," she says to the windshield.

The gravel crunches beneath the tires as she rolls onto the King George. Traffic is quiet this time of night.

She arrives at the Golden Arches and pulls into the drive thru. After placing the brown bag with the Big Mac and fries on the passenger seat and the drink in the cup holder, she collects her change. *What I wouldn't do for a Gin and Tonic.* She gets back onto the King George and a block so familiar. Her childhood haunt, she remembers when they widened the highway to four lanes. Progress, development, spaces taken—The Milk Jug, the Country Kitchen—gone. Replaced and built over—always up, higher, wider, bigger, brighter, and faster. The Sky Train. The traffic lights. The highway. Apartments and condos are everywhere fields and pastures and forest used to be. Glitz and glam replacing soil and trees. All those trails and tree forts are gone. She rolls her gum into a napkin and drops it, careful to keep her eyes on the road, and pulls out a tangle of fries, shoving them into her mouth. The crispy outer layer gives way to the fluffy inside. She chews, moans softly.

The car lurches, launching her food bag onto the floor. She turns the stiffening wheel and gets the car to the curb, it stalls, red light colours the dash and the power steering completely gives out.

Nora exhales, rests her head on the wheel and closes her eyes.

The adoptive parents entered the delivery room without knocking. They wore long felt overcoats that stretched below their knees. His was grey, hers beige. Nora stared at their puffy, sky-blue shoe covers, like little clouds around their feet. She had written a name on a slip of paper and thought about sharing it with them, but that would involve eye contact.

"This is God's baby," they said.

Nora squeezes the wheel. The greasy lump of food in her stomach.

Thump, thump, thump. Again, it's Maggie rapping the driver's door. She motions for Nora to roll the window down.

"Happy Birthday, Nora, party's over."

Maggie opens the car door and on goes the interior light.

"Nice shoes."

They look at the Crocs.

"And my jacket. Get out." She points at Joan's car. "I'll get your food."

Once they buckle in, Nora asks Maggie to take her to Ada's complex. "Please?"

"No," Maggie says, shaking her head. She looks over at Nora. The redness in Nora's cheeks has faded. The blood is gone. Maggie continues south on the King George. Her cell phone rings. "What the hell am I supposed to tell Terwott?"

"Nothing," Nora says. "Don't answer."

Nora holds her Big Mac and chews, savouring the Thousand Islands dressing and the sesame seed bun, crunching out the last fry bits, salty and soaked with grease.

"You've got five minutes."

"Okay, you've got five minutes at Ada's complex."

"Five minutes," Nora echoes, lowering her window and the glass drops inside the door, *clunk*. "Oh," Nora says. "That didn't sound good. I only wanted to reach out for a handful of rain."

Moist outside air whips into the car lifting the MacDonald's bag. Nora reaches for it and misses. The bag floats into the back seat.

They drive until they reach the high-rise.

Ada sold the family home. The three-acre parcel of land went to Sand and Associates, 'We are where you want to live' for seven figures. They built The Willow, a fifteen-story apartment complex, encircling the tree that once stood in front of her childhood home. The tree is like a massive head of unkempt hair, hanging over the eyes, waiting for someone to swipe it aside. She climbed it as a kid and threw blackberries at the boys riding bikes below. That was when her life was weekends and mischief. The city passed a bylaw that prohibits the planting of willows. The root system runs too deep, constantly searching for water, penetrating foundations, drain systems, and even buckling driveways. They ruin so much staying alive.

Frameless panes of glass, and the bright light projecting from inside, make the high-rise look like a giant movie screen. Nora feels like she's arrived at the drive-in. One after another the apartment doors are visible through the glass, stuck in an assembly line awaiting an addition, a colourful touch to set them apart. But it never happens. Every door's the same, every floor the same, bookended with potted plastic trees, standing below a red exit sign in a building crammed with tenants. The apartments sold out in a record three days.

Maggie and Nora stand in the foyer and stare at the video intercom. A glossy camera eye stares back. Maggie finds an Ada Park in the directory and presses the call button. A red light appears below the camera.

"My God, Nora? Is that you?"

"Ada?"

"It's one o'clock in the morning!"

Apologizing, Nora explains that she came from the hospital to find out more about her adopted son.

"That was years ago."

"There's nothing you can tell me?" Nora asks, leaning toward the camera.

"I do have a photo... somewhere. Hold on."

Ada's voice returns. "I'll bring it down."

Nora turns to Maggie who lifts her arms and lets them flop against her sides. They walk to the elevators and watch the hall lantern tick down 15-14-13... and stop on L. Out steps Ada in a floral dressing gown, holding a framed photo. A young man in his mid-twenties stands with Ada next to a Denny's restaurant sign. Taller than Ada, his blue jeans, rolled into a four-inch cuff, rest above sockless feet and tan suede shoes.

"No socks," Nora says, her finger tracing the cold metal frame. "Chic."

Most of his bangs are tucked behind his ears, but a thick spear of hair sits on his cheek. He's leaning back, mid laugh, carefree, in a body that continued to grow and age. Nora imagines him aging backward in a sort of fictional flip book. Smiling and crying, red-faced and mad, asking to take the car to Cultus Lake for the weekend—denied. Sneaking out to drink beer behind Georges Vanier Elementary and being brought home by the cops with a bloody face. Images fly, the boy getting smaller, dressing for Halloween, opening Christmas presents, and skating at the Newton Arena. From riding his ten-speed, back to a tricycle, back to his first steps, to feeding himself from a plastic bowl that rests on the kitchen table. Back to that little bundle at the home for unwed mothers, sated and sleeping on her breast. She wants to experience it all—somehow, someway. But she can't.

"His name?"

"Oh, Nora," Ada says, "its's been so long now, and it was the briefest of visits. I don't remember."

Nora gives the photo back to Ada, resting a hand on hers so they both touch the photo. "Harper," Nora says, remembering the name she had scribbled down. "I bet it was Harper James."

"No," Ada says, pulling her hand away. "That wasn't it."

"Well, it had to be something."

Nora turns to look at the willow in front of the complex, with its lance-shaped leaves, and rough, grey, ridged bark, and remembers that from the crown she could see every house in the neighbourhood and hear all the other children's voices. She stayed up there for hours. No one found her.

"Forget it, Nora." Maggie places a hand on her shoulder and leaves it there, "Time to go."

Nora moves closer to the window; it's quiet on the foyer carpet. She misses the sound of her Crocs on the asphalt and blackberry-stained hands. She blinks, unable to recognize her own reflection in the glass.

BLOWING ACROSS THE TOP

SHE SITS IN ONE of the five chairs at the front of the line with a flute on her lap and a phone in her hand, waiting to perform. Maya wore her ankle-length black dress to her Spring Recital. She stares at what's behind the pulpit, a giant window, the coloured plastic panels that play with the light. Looking at all those colours, she can't tell if it's cloudy, raining, or sunny outside. One blue panel has a spiderweb crack across its surface.

"Mama, I'm nervous."

Her mother brushes a hair from Maya's shoulder.

"That's normal. You got this. Oh look, love, he's back."

Her mother points at Steve, Maya's stepdad, with her eyebrows up, as if she wants Maya to recognize his value. Maya saw him earlier, on the front steps of Our Lady of Good Counsel, searching for a stronger signal. She looks at his Facebook post, instead of him, a burst of photos of Maya and her mother from a recent outdoor rehearsal. She notices Steve doesn't have many followers. A deep blue sky and bright skin, he probably chose *Dramatic Cool* for the photo filter. Maya shares the photos with her dad.

"Did you invite him?"

"Who? Steve?"

"No. Dad."

"We've talked about this. Steve doesn't want him here."

"I know. They don't have to sit together."

Her mother frowns. "And you *really* think he'll show?"

"If you talk to him, and tell him to *please* come, he might."

"Sometimes, talking doesn't fix things."

"But he could help. He's done this before."

"It's not that easy."

"But if he were here—"

"Enough."

Her mother raises her hands.

"Remember, I am not staying long."

She turns and walks toward the first pew.

"I'm leaving right after you perform. Steve's taking you home."

Maya texts her father the invite.

Her mother moves in next to Steve on the worn oak bench. The wood stain lightens at the contact points, like old jeans at the knees. All those sliding backsides have given it some comfort. They are wedged in next to all the other families, shoulder-to-shoulder and thigh-to-thigh. Everyone paid $25 to see their kid play. Those with no room to sit, stand next to the wall. The place is packed.

Maya scrolls her phone for her dad's reply but finds nothing. Her music teacher approaches wearing a hand-it-over look. Maya quickly swipes right, powers down, and holds her phone up for her to grab, but not without an eye roll.

Maya's in line behind a guitarist, two pianists, and a drummer—all ten and under. She counts a hundred people in the audience. Her father's not there. Her left hand trembles. She tells herself she's played the song on her flute that many times: a hundred. She picks it up. She imagines playing for each audience member, one by one. They smile at her trills, her movement across the keys, her embouchure. But a thought creeps in: *What if I blow it?* She laughs. *What if I don't?*

Tommy is in his apartment when he spots the photos of Maya and his ex-wife Joanne on his News Feed. He reads her invite and looks at the photos, adding a like, a love, and a heart-eyed emoji, before he pushes off.

Tommy has no laces in his shoes. He is using one to tie off. Staring at the skin on his wrist, he feels for a large vein. Gently, over and over, he presses it, leaving a fading white fingerprint as it expands. Holding a loaded syringe parallel to his arm, *c'mon,* Tommy slides the bevel deep into his vein, and on the pull, blood clouds the barrel—he's sure he's in.

Be there for me.

After the push, he removes the needle, dropping it on the carpet, and loosens the lace. His heart pulses, and this new blood mix washes him back into the soft sofa cushions. Tommy's lips part. He draws air in through his teeth. He thinks about the recital, Maya preparing to go on—she must be nervous, afraid even, like he is now. He exhales.

Last time they were together, Tommy left her unaccompanied on the bus. She ended up at the Newton terminus two hours later, lost and upset, her phone dead. Maya and her father have not gone anywhere together since last April. Tommy's never invited; Maya's not allowed.

About two months ago, he broke into his old home and took Steve's entire comic book collection, including an *Amazing Spider-Man* #27 valued at $10,000, and pawned it all. Before taking the comics, he wandered around all the rooms. He tapped the glass on the fish tank, spooking the fish. He stopped in Maya's room, picked clothes from the floor, dropped them in the hamper, and reorganized some books on her desk. He put his favourite, *The Giving Tree*, on top. He went into the master bedroom, clicked on the light in the walk-in closet and, partly hidden by hanging dresses, he spotted a cardboard box. He placed it on the bed, unfolded the major and minor flaps and rifled through the contents. Comics, bagged and in chronological order. Tommy had trouble riding his bike with the box, and crossing the lawn he almost dropped it.

The same day Steve buzzed Tommy on his apartment intercom.

"I know it was you."

"Your fucking comic book collection?" Tommy laughed, but not because it was funny, because the truth can embolden.

"You're telling me I took your comics and traded them all for a couple points of junk."

"Well, uh, you know where the spare key is, and what they're worth."

"Jo never married you for your brains. You're a landscaper. She just hired you to see someone back in the yard."

Then Joanne called Tommy. She said she refused to go to the police, even though Mrs. Mackenzie, a neighbour, saw him in the yard, balancing a box on the handlebars.

"Return them, Tom. No questions asked."

"What if I don't have 'em anymore?"

Sometimes, Tommy sits at the bus shelter across the street from the family home. He watches Steve cut the lawn, fix the eaves, and rev up the leaf blower that he parades around on his back while swinging the blow tube: the sound rattles the kitchen window, and sometimes interrupts his phone conversations with Maya.

"When are *you* coming home?"

"For now, it's Phone only, MyMy. Give it time. We'll get to see more of each other soon. How's that flute? If you open the basement window, I bet I can hear you practise."

"You can?"

Tommy pulls on his blue hoodie with a faded Pepsi logo before leaving his apartment. He used to be a flautist, and now he's going to his daughter's first performance. He rides the bus—Joanne calls it "the loser cruiser." He lost his car in the same accident that disfigured his body and face with third-degree burns. The scar tissue made playing impossible. He had been drinking. It was Oktoberfest and he drove home. He was on the King George when he crossed the centerline. The collision with the oncoming vehicle ruptured the fuel line. He was unconscious and buckled in, while the car fire blazed. The first responders were quick, but sixty percent of his body burned. After treatment he was discharged from the Burn Unit with an oxycodone dependency and a promise to be monitored.

The growth of new nerve endings meant constant pain, and he replaced oxy with heroin.

On the bus he's cold, even with warm air blowing from the vent. When he's like this, Tommy usually forgets where he's going, that he's a teacher, a musician, and a father... but today he wants to remember.

When he spots the sign for Hawthorne Park, he yanks the signal cord. He knows how to get to the church. The fresh air does little to bring him down. He enters the church high as a kite, drifting through parents, the kids waiting to go on, and people standing next to the pews. With his hood up, it's hard to see his face; he makes his way to the front, he gets a wide berth. After the accident people stared at the scars that formed to repair the wounds. Over time they have faded, flattened and softened, but his face remains a patchwork of skin grafts.

Maya's about to go on. Tommy is certain she recognizes his Pepsi hoodie, the soft creases at the elbows from all the washings, it was a Father's Day gift. On stage, five-year-old Holden Mendez is making the drum beat dance. Tommy sways next to a lectern, adjusting his feet to maintain balance. His jeans have a rear pocket hanging off, like an opened ear of corn, revealing a dark patch of denim underneath.

Tommy looks at all the people: a field of stars he can't touch or rearrange. He's the centre, they pulse from dim to bright, moving in and out, circling him over time, like star trails in a time-lapsed photo of the night sky. Tommy's arms and legs are heavy, everything droops—his eyes are half-hooded, closing blinds. He lifts his chin to the applause, his lips twitch a smile, but they're not clapping for him.

"Thank you very much, Holden Mendez," calls the MC. "Hey, little man," he points a finger, "you certainly can keep that beat."

Holden, fitted with a red bow tie and squeezing his red drumsticks, bows at center stage.

"Now, please welcome Maya Pearson and her flute. She is performing Hatikvah for you this afternoon."

Tommy moves closer. Most of him's in slow motion; his head sinks low then rises with a start, like he's struggling to stay awake. With his laces gone, his shoes clomp the wood floor.

It's his Yamaha flute in Maya's hands. He had to save up to buy it, a year of delivering papers and chopping firewood. And in Grade 12 he received the provincial medal for excellence from the Royal Conservatory of Canada.

Tommy showed her how to clean the three silvery sections with a soft rag wrapped around the cleaning rod. Walking her through the assembly, he slid and twisted the head, body and foot piece into one.

"When you play, keep both elbows up a little, up like this, and the barrel down slightly. Thumb goes here."

Tommy had pressed his bottom lip onto the lip plate. "It's like blowing across the top of a bottle."

That lesson was three years ago.

She places the sheet of music on the stand.

She moves her foot, *tap, tap, tap,* and nods, cueing her piano accompaniment. When she lifts her elbow to play, her music sheet drops, swinging back and forth, like a fallen leaf. It lands near Tommy.

Tommy takes two steps and picks up the paper, folds it lengthwise and snaps it flat.

He hands the music to the MC.

"Thank you, sir. Let's get that back where it belongs."

Maya has her father's slate grey eyes. She wipes them and clears her throat.

Again, she taps her foot, again the piano plays.

Tommy closes his eyes to listen. Maya's breath moves through the barrel, her fingers press the right keys, the notes are low and sombre, and for a moment everyone in that room breathes together. Her tone is just right—soft, then loud, then soft, and finally silent.

WHEN WOMEN SHOOT

AT TWENTY-SIX Dean Witherspoon was tall and thin, like a bent pipe cleaner stuffed into his seat at the arena. Olive skin and grey eyes were topped with a wave of thick black hair. He toggled between "real" life, a cell phone screen, and the Jumbo Tron. With the world laid out in triple, he settled for the version on the big screen, with the largest image and the highest resolution. It brought the things he wanted closer.

A stream of people came on to the ice through the Zamboni door and she was the last. Blonde and cropped, her hair was like a helmet, but she wore Stan Smiths and jeans torn at the knees—new denim, made to look old. He raised his phone, zoomed in and tapped record. He imagined sitting with her at the game, his arm hanging off her shoulder, her hand draped over his knee, like a regular couple. Well, a regular couple who just met. But in fact, she was strapped to the back of an ATV with a CO_2 canister against her thigh, cradling a T-shirt gun. With her back to the driver, she looked like Charlize Theron crossing the desert in that movie. Was she always this fearless? Is anyone?

Her driver, in a helmet and goggles, fishtailed around the face-off dot, hunched over and white knuckled. They stopped at the hash marks. She waved to the crowd, trying to generate excitement before she shouldered her gun. The driver held the clutch, snapped her wrist, and filled the air with more blue smoke.

Dean could make out a set of Roman numerals etched into the nape of her neck, a numerical tattoo, MCMXLIX. A year? 1949. The year Dean's mother was born. Dean stared at the empty seat, where his mom should be, but "Get out! Leave me alone!" had ended their last conversation. He looked down at his wrist and the purple bruise below his thumb. Pushed out, and in her haste, she slammed the door on his hand.

Dean powered down and pocketed his phone, stood, and shook out his hand, ready for whatever flew his way. Normally, hockey fans would do anything for a T-shirt. It was like a baton in the hands of a blue-collar conductor charged with bringing the stadium to life, but most of the fans at this game faced their phones, drunk with cellular connections. They snapped selfies and wished for longer arms to capture even more. A guy beside Dean texted, "You won't believe where I am right now!" Dean spotted her again, barreling across the ice on rubber tires.

She fired.

Ka-thunk!

A beer-can sized bullet of cotton climbed to the upper decks of Rogers Arena. Dean followed it, his head on a swivel. A T-shirt gun was an interesting science topic: The chemistry of the gun. *Remember class, speed is equal to distance divided by time. How did that projectile travel that far? That fast?* He could create an exam with questions that drew attention to the specifics, provide the formulae, and set it up in a hockey rink. He would name-drop his favourite players, even if the students didn't recognize any.

He continued to watch her first shot, like it was a fight developing behind the play. He waited for it to peak and descend. Meanwhile, she moved to centre ice and the left tire clipped the roll of carpet used for the anthem singer. She squeezed the gun to keep it from bouncing loose and tapped the trigger. And something so easily done, released the energy in that gun.

Kathunk!

The second shot cleared the plexiglass *and* the netting, and struck Dean in the jaw, like an enforcer's power punch. *Whack!* It twisted his head even further from the play. The T-shirt bullet was more than compressed cotton.

Orca Bay had slipped in a logo'd puck—six ounces of vulcanized rubber was buried inside each shirt.

Go Canucks Go!

Dean lost his balance, bounced off a man to his right, and fell forward. With the steep incline of seats, his fall was like a step from a cliff. He tumbled over two rows, sending nachos, salmon rolls and beer everywhere, like liquid confetti tossed in celebration of his arrival. And like the confetti, he found the floor. They replayed the fall on the Jumbo Tron. Dean watched it from between seats and legs, without a free hand to cover his eyes, and the crowd erupted like someone had scored. *Can you believe it? Did you see that?*

Up above, in the press box, some guy on the ownership team wrote this down: *The more humiliation the better*. At the end of the replay, with food and drink splattered everywhere, there was a moment when the cheer became a groan, because West Coast Salmon Rolls were $12, and the Granville Island Pale Ale was $18. The big screen blanked and glitched, but the collective demand for more was strong, so most went back to their handhelds.

Dean lay with his cheek on the concrete. His arms and legs splayed like branches from a fallen tree. Recognizing the chance, some in the crowd moved closer. One man stepped onto a seat back, steadied himself on a fan in front, lifted and angled his phone for a better shot. After he took a few, a woman offered hers up, "Get one for me? Please?"

Dean wanted everyone to know it wasn't a dive staged for the cameras, and that soon enough he would be out, down for the count, off in la-la land, because he could feel this world slipping like a puck between his pads. And one more thing: if they posted it, could his face be pixeled out? He didn't want anyone to worry, especially his mom.

At that moment, caught between consciousness and beyond, Dean felt like he was watching a film about himself—lately his life was hard. His mother, Colleen, had depression. Her withdrawal, seclusion, and the talking-to-herself had worsened. He stopped in daily, and heard her from behind the closed door, in a heated monologue about all that had gone wrong. She talked as if someone was listening.

"I don't need everyone's love," his mother would say. "Only a handful of good people."

The last conversation she had with her ex-husband was stuck on replay and she sought a better ending. She was in constant rehearsal, waiting for the right words to surface—a zinger, a showstopper, that would have changed the outcome.

The neighbours watched from narrow openings in curtained windows and listened through cracked front doors, motivated by the desire to verify the picture they had of a woman falling apart. Sometimes they leaned over the fence or called from the neighbouring driveway when Dean climbed the steps, "Hey Deano, have you got a minute? Is she okay? Does she talk like that often?"

What could he say? What could he tell them? One thing was clear: they wanted him to do something to make her stop. Fear of aberrance, dressed up as kindness.

Her obscenity-filled monologues, were often a microscopic look at failure. This from a woman who never swore in public, insisted on good manners, and always used please and thank you. Now, the fabric under her arms sweat stained, her face had a grey pallor, and her hair was matted in circles. No longer making the weekly trip to have her hair done at June's Hair Salon. The best Dean could do was pick up the empty wine bottles, toss them in the recycle bin and change her bedding, all done to a soft chorus of, "No, look, I'm fine. I'm tired. Don't touch that."

"Have you eaten today?"

Dean's question was met with a deadpan stare that said, *What does that have to do with anything?*

Dean was convinced that having to care for the family, for him, his little brother and sister and his dad; having to put dinner on the table every damn night, make lunches, wash dishes, do laundry, vacuum, plus her nursing job at the Thompson House—it all drove crazy to the front door.

Maybe her troubles began before the arrival of the children, when his father took this young woman who had arrived on a plane from Scotland and made her into a wife. Dean wondered what a goodbye like that was like, leaving family and her Isle of Skye, with its jagged peaks and shores of black sand.

"You lost something moving to Canada," his father would say, "and somehow that's my fault? Get your shit together, Colleen."

Working full time as a nurse didn't help: the compassion fatigue, the burnout. Older now, Dean recognized her burden. His father had high standards, like he was a CEO of some Fortune 500 company—which he wasn't. He worked construction off and on, mostly off. He ate his meals late and always over the sink. He wanted things just so, and if they weren't, well look out, the doors slammed, and Colleen was thrown to the floor along with her things. And as kids, they watched, and listened, uncertain, afraid, getting to their rooms, under the bed, anywhere that breathing wouldn't give them away.

The last time Dean spoke to his father he held the frying pan head high, soap suds trailing down his arm and dripping from his elbow.

"Touch her again and I swear to God."

Dean was fifteen.

And after two decades of marriage, his father pulled the rug right out—he left his wife for the receptionist at

Super Cuts. The new couple moved to Manitoba, in much the same way the school year ends, and the kids leave for summer holidays. How could his mom compete with someone new? Two weeks ago, on social media, Colleen learned that he remarried and there was a new baby boy, a stepbrother for the whole family to meet. She didn't know where to place that information, so it wouldn't hurt like hell.

"He hasn't done a damn thing to support this family. Not a red cent. And he's trying all over?"

Dean woke at Vancouver General and stared at the green walls of the ICU. He was alone in a room for four. He was concussed and told to keep the lights low and stay off technology. It didn't matter. He couldn't find his phone anyway.

The hospital was sound: IV-pump alarms, and loudspeakers that buzzed with, "Doctor Halpern to Admissions. Doctor Halpern Admissions". Plus other demands for people to report here or there. The intercom was like a GPS for suffering.

A Pine-Sol aroma filled Dean's room. He had a fractured rib, a bruised cheek, and a blood shot eye.

When the meds wore off, his face stayed swollen and throbbed with each heartbeat. The injury made chewing impossible. He sat up, pulled the overbed table closer and stabbed a straw into a styrofoam cup, lifted it and sucked at the lukewarm puree. It felt like a litre. He closed his eyes and imagined a plate of baby back ribs, stacked high and smothered in BBQ sauce, burned black from the grill and served with baked potato, sour cream and chives. No use, the puree still tasted like crap. He swiped the cup into the trash.

"You'll need it," the nurse said entering the room, "to get stronger."

Dean wrote, *I'll take my chances,* on the notepad the nurse had given him. He turned to show it.

And turned it back to write more, *Could I try jello again? And I can't find my phone anywhere. Was it on me when I arrived?*

"Sure," the nurse said. "I'll get the jello and ask about the phone."

Thanks.

Dean thought about his class, the marking—Jesus, the marking. And the report cards to complete... he was still learning the template, all those numbers and no room for individual comments. He could see the pile of English assignments and science tests, needy fingers poking to wake him from a nap.

He looked for a phone and thought about calling his brother on Vancouver Island, or his sister in Calgary, but they were so far away and of little help. The thought of having to walk them through the events and respond to their questions, it would be like another parent-teacher interview.

When she walked in, Dean's breath caught.

She stood by his bed. Her eyes were a Facebook blue.

"I'm not supposed to be here," she said quickly. "I've been told not to come, and especially *not* to apologize," deepening her voice. "No individual correspondence can be entered into, remember an apology may be seen as an admission of guilt."

She said she didn't care. She wanted to be sure he was okay.

"I thought I killed you," her shoulders slackened. "But you're fine," she exhaled. "Right?"

She lay a hand on the bed.

He turned to a new page in his notepad and wrote, *Hello! My name is Dean.*

"Oh, right," she said extending a hand. "Kelly Loughlin." Her hand was soft and cool, and her perfume overtook the Pine-Sol. Around her neck was a black checkered scarf.

Dean wrote more on his pad: *You haven't really apologized yet.*

He turned the pad. She read it and smiled, again.

"So," she said, crossing her arms and feigning anger, "this is how it's going to be, eh? You don't really want to hear that, do you?"

But Dean did, he wanted recognition for his pain and suffering.

You didn't mean to shoot me. Did you? Dean wrote.

"Well, I don't know," she brought her fingers to her mouth, "now that we've met." She laughed.

She continued to talk, and he listened. A Simon Fraser University student completing a bachelor's degree in Kinesiology, she was on her way to being a physiotherapist. She worked on the T-shirt crew to cover tuition. She rented a basement apartment in Port Moody, riding her bike up the mountain trails every day.

"I save on parking."

"Even in the rain?"

"Love the rain, and the mud, and the shower."

She visited him regularly over the next three days.

Dean was on to solid food and he could talk again, but it was difficult. At times he would struggle to find the correct word. He knew what he wanted to say, but it wouldn't come out right. Moments of temporary confusion the doctor called it. And the headaches were monumental. Dean was scheduled for discharge in four days. Kelly agreed to give him a ride home.

On the fourth day, while Dean waited for her to show, he was given the green light for screen time, so he watched a local report on the beach town of White Rock. He imagined having coffee with her in warmer weather. The crowds, the sunshine, and the smell of the ocean. The report featured a winter storm surge that had damaged the local pier. Freed boats, like torpedoes, crashed over and over into the mid-point of the span and took out a thirty-metre section of decking. One man had walked to the end of the quarter-mile span, before the waves had bashed that section apart. A rescue team had been dispatched to get him back onto Marine Drive.

Barnacle-encrusted pilings that once held the pier poked from the water, no longer supporting anything. The guy was on the wrong side. Sheets of rain whipped the shore.

"He's still stranded out there," came the reporter's calm voice, "and it doesn't look like the storm will end any time soon. A rescue helicopter is en route. We'll have more as the story unfolds. Back to you."

Kelly never showed and Dean was told he had to stay another day, pending the results of his MRI.

That night he dreamt he was stranded on a pier, waiting for a medic and the rescue harness to drop from the Cormorant helicopter. Once the medic came down the load line, and rested his feet firmly on the deck, he handed Dean the harness. Dean slipped it on and heard the carabiner's *click* before they twisted and twirled their way up to the fuselage, but Dean sunk lower and fell into the cold water. The sting of the water had him sitting upright in his bed and calling for the nurse.

The following day Kelly walked into the hospital room with a tall, bearded guy, mid-twenties, the same age as Dean.

"This is Noah."

More alarms sounded from a neighbouring room.

"My boyfriend," she added.

Noah looked like a GAP mannequin, a forced smile was held up by the corners of his mouth, and he wore grey slacks, a soft green utility jacket, and zippered leather boots. Dean was the customer staring through the window.

"Oh," Dean said in a raspy voice, "a boyfriend, I mean your boyfriend."

Dean addressed him, "Careful, bud," pointing at her with his thumb. "This one's dangerous. You might end up in here like me."

"This is the fucking guy?" Noah asked. Stepping closer to the bed. There was a pause, the type that meant discomfort.

"Yep," Dean said looking to Kelly and then Noah, eyebrows up. "I'm the fucking guy."

"I don't know," Noah said, leaning forward. "I expected someone bigger."

Kelly told Noah to go get them a coffee.

"I'll meet you in the cafeteria in 15 minutes."

He left.

"What happened?" Dean asked. "You didn't show yesterday."

"I pulled an all-nighter. It was a term paper. I was in no shape to drive."

"That only applies when you've had too much to drink."

"I called the hospital today and was surprised to hear that you were still here. When are you leaving?"

"They found something on the MRI."

"What?"

"Not sure. I'm meeting the doctor," Dean glanced at the clock on the wall, "in about 10 minutes."

"Oh."

"You don't need to keep coming here. It's kind, but unnecessary."

"Well," her face flushed, "here's my number," she handed him a business card. "I really am sorry about what happened. Maybe you'll call me when you're out?"

"Maybe."

She left and the doctor arrived.

"Your results."

The doctor drew the bed curtain, even though they were alone.

"The bad news. Your scan shows a golf-ball sized tumour that is pressing into your cerebellum," she pointed to the back of her own head and waited, placing a manila folder on the bed. "The good news. I'm not sure who shot that puck, but you were lucky, we wouldn't have found it otherwise. We can get it out. Some of the symptoms you may have noticed, even before the accident, like difficulty with balance, flickering of the eyes, and trouble speaking."

"Tell me again—how am I lucky?"

Dean rubbed the back of his head. His hair felt like the bristles on an old toothbrush. The thought of a tumour there, a part of him, brought up bile in the back of his throat. The bitter taste made him swallow. If he had a surgeon's blade and a mirror positioned right, could he carve it out himself, like coring an apple?

"We'll meet tomorrow to arrange your pre-op. In the meantime, is there someone you can call? A family member?"

"Ya, I guess."

"I know it's not the kind of conversation you want right now, but you need to talk to someone."

The doctor slid the curtain open and left the room. Her footsteps were soft on the linoleum floor.

Dean went quiet. He let it wrap him, and his head sunk deeper into the pillow. With his teeth grinding, a rage was building. Anger is stronger than fear.

He heard a faint whistling moving closer to his room. A melody he didn't know, a tune in sharp contrast to the buzz and beep of hospital sounds. Noah walked in with two large coffees, stopped whistling and stood at the foot of Dean's bed.

"Hey, maybe I was kind of a dick earlier. You like coffee?"

Noah placed one cup on the table.

“I hope you’re better soon and get outta this fucking place.”

“Thanks.”

Noah turned and left.

Dean reached for the coffee and hit it with the back of his hand, knocking it off the table. The lid popped and coffee flowed onto the floor.

“Jesus.”

He sat up in bed and lifted the covers, his pale skin magnifying the dark circles under his eyes and the bruises. He swung his feet to the floor and stood in his hospital gown, dizzy from the quickness of it all. He wheeled the table clear of the coffee puddle widening on the floor, grabbed the cup and lid and held an open hand underneath to catch the drips, tossing it all into the garbage.

The nurse returned. “Everything okay?”

“Sorry about the mess,” Dean said walking into the bathroom. “I’m going to wash my hands.”

“No problem, I’ll get that cleaned up.”

“Oh, before I forget,” she reached into her pocket, talking louder so he could hear as he closed the bathroom door, “Your phone. I’ll put it on the nightstand.”

Dean returned to bed, picked up his phone, and tapped it with his thumb. The screen flickered, the glow lit up his face.

He sat on the bed and dialed her number.

“Mom. It’s me.” There was a pause. “I know, me too. Listen, I have something to tell you.”

HIT SUBMIT

THIRTY-SIX TERM papers stand between Sam and the end of the winter semester. A giant palm on the forehead, pushing him into his chair, drowning him. What if he doesn't grade them? Will Catherine Essar and the rest of Student Services come knocking? Her email is friendly enough, a reminder of today's deadline and *Happy Holidays in spite of it all!* But Sam knows she counts herself among those who believe that college professors, even new ones like Sam Anderson, sit on their asses all day and night, then go on holiday. Could he lose his job? Go on, buzz the front door, stand at a distance, in your mask, and wave the collective agreement till your arm sprains. Sam's apartment is tiny, but he knows where to hide.

His students are different. Sam feels responsible for them. His inbox fills with messages, like that scene from

Harry Potter when the mail won't stop. They start with... "I have a question" or "I'm not sure if you can answer this" or "I know you're busy"—but they all end the same: "Did you grade my paper?" As though he's reclining on a Cuban beach, heels in the sand, sipping his third Mojito, and needs a reminder. He's certain he can submit the grades in the next six hours. He has to.

Sam locks eyes with his computer. "Damn the torpedoes!" Let the point, click, and drag begin, especially the drag. Get it over with. Isn't that what his students say? Sure, there'll be a few good ones, maybe, but most are dedicated, solemn entries in the shit show. Sign here and here. Can you blame them? The pandemic is the angry mob breaching the front door, dumping desk drawers, rifling through personal belongings, searching for something good to screw you with. Sam checks the numbers—cases up, hospitalizations up, but the ICUs are down. He knows it's because people die. Isn't that why they call it the dead of winter?

Sam is twenty-four and he sublets a 1½ in Notre-Dame-de-Grace. Like Dostoevsky in exile—with a desk, a window, and winter blowing in. The Old Orchard Manor: it sounds like a retirement home, and during lockdown it is. His hand hovers above the steam radiator; unconvinced, he tugs on another sweater. When the building went up, he wonders, did they even remember winter?

From his desk he watches lit-up snow fall from a streetlamp and wishes the world could stop and start on a different day. But the flakes fall. Some track sideways and others float on currents that carry them up and out of view. As a kid, he pulled black paper from the freezer and ran outside to catch them, like a waiter in reverse. His mother stood on the doorstep, reminding him to take note of their needle, column, plate, and rime. Their sharp details brought to bear against black. He learned that no two snowflakes are alike.

How did he get here? Even with so much alone time, he let his academic responsibilities slide, along with the self-imposed deadlines. COVID time bleed. Hours of gaming, waves of regret, and a completion rate of 71% on Marvel's Spider Man—that's all he can show. Well, that and the realization that teaching is not for him. Trying to run a classroom in the chaos. Having to be *on*, all the time, when everything else is so off. A dog's breakfast.

Sam clicks the blue desktop folder to ready the first paper, rotates his head, locks then flexes his fingers, holding them for the *crack*. He parks the cursor in a screen corner and reads aloud, "The nature of the attention one brings to bear on anything alters what one finds." He reads it again, then scrolls back to the title page. Did that line come from this eighteen-year-old mind? He notes the name, Kimberly Meadows—she sounds like an outdoor-clothing line. He changes platforms to scan her photo.

The students wear masks in class, so the online self-portraits are useless. He recognizes no one. The world is a giant bank heist, and we're all getting robbed.

During class Sam goes maskless, unafraid of the shared air, so they all recognize him, his only brush with fame. But when their masks lower for a drink or a nose scratch and the rest of their face appears, it's out of whack. Whether it's a Roman nose, a rubbery curve to the chin, or pencil lips, something's way off. Who are these people? Sam's convinced it's the closest he's come to a hallucination. Over the past four months, he has met them twice a week, for an hour and a half; they're still strangers.

He reviews Kimberly's record. She's missed more classes than she's attended and landed in the 'student at risk' column with an overall average of 48%. Sam pinches the bridge of his nose and reads her opening line again, but the brilliance remains. The idea is not referenced. It sits there, the last peanut in the bowl. He scrolls the rest of the paper, the structure, format, page numbers, and APA referencing are bang on. This is *the* Hail Mary. Sam clicks the similarity report, and the result is a whopping 87%. He adjusts, sliding forward in his chair. The passages lifted from online sources are highlighted in different colours and include source details. The main one is Jonas Hartwig, Sam's former student. The net widens.

"What a pain in the ass."

Filling a plagiarism report takes time and it's worse than grading a bad paper: the form, the screen shots, then the meeting with the dean. The backdrop for the entire process is whether to fail, which isn't a tough call when the only way to grade is down. Finally, there's the confrontation. Seldom does a full confession come, instead students double down. "Gimme a break. I would never cheat. I have no idea what you're talking about." But faced with the evidence, they buckle. "I'm sorry. Can we work something out? What about my university standing? My transcript? There's this program I want to get into, and you'll ruin that." The gaslighting begins.

He opens a different paper, longing for a goofy intro line, and he's rewarded. "Since the dawn of time humans have wondered about the mind." He adjusts his posture, sliding back into a comfy part of the chair. "Hell ya," Sam says. "Tell me about it." Now this is a paper that he can get behind. Mistakes, sure, some grammatical errors, no problem, he highlights them and populates the rubric with numbers and a little praise. Maybe there's some beauty in mediocrity, in the familiar, and a little comfort too. He's on a roll and grades five more papers, but he must contact Kimberly and Jonas, it's college policy. He sends Kimberly a message and cc's Jonas, "Why does your paper have a similarity score of 87% with most of it identical to the work of Jonas Hartwig?" The power of a rhetorical question.

Through the shared wall of his apartment, Sam hears voices rage. It's Kaylee and Réjean—the couple in 4B. He glances at his watch; forget the time, what day is it? It's Friday, 7:00 p.m., so they've probably had dinner, it's usually casual talk and music, often kicked off with The Cure singing, "Friday I'm in love." Followed by the rhythmic *thump* of the headboard—Sam's cue to don the noise-cancelling headphones. He knows so much about his neighbours, a by-product of a world forced together, but tonight, no music. Instead, someone is knocked to the floor, and they bang and tumble into the shared wall. Then there are several sharp slaps or punches. Together, apart, together, apart. Then a scream, and it's Sam who stops breathing.

He stands. Should he go next door, ring the bell and ask, "Is everything okay?" He decides yes. Standing at their apartment door, in slippers and sweatpants, he leans in to hear better. Nothing. His thumb lightly circles the ringer, clearing the dust from the white plastic, but he knocks hard instead. One, two, three. His heart beats like a punch.

The door cracks. Kaylee's face appears in the shadow. They often exchange a nod and a smile, when sharing an elevator or tossing junk mail. They also talk about Kaylee and Réjean's restaurant or Sam's classes. Sam knows the restaurant is gone. He passes it on his walk to the train, *À Louer* emblazoned across the bay window. Signs like that pop up every day. Neighbourhood restaurants were the first to go, along with customers, staff, and their livelihood. COVID smears the familiar.

"Everything okay in there?" he asks.

She leans into the hall. Her face is puffed red, the distorted expression is a snapshot of fear.

"Of course," she responds. "Are you eavesdropping? What the fuck is wrong with you?"

"Oh, I just thought—"

"Well don't." She closes the door.

Sam clears his throat and walks down the hall to check his laundry. He unties, tightens, and reties the drawstring on his sweats.

Welcome to lockdown. The prison analogy is no accident. *Please avoid leaving home and do so only when essential.* Isn't everything essential? Groceries? Human contact? Compassion? Escape? When he arrives at the room, someone has removed his clothes from the washer and put them on top of the dryer. The pile—more sweatpants, towels, dress socks, underwear, and his ex Josée's Radiohead T-shirt, are all coiled into a cold, wet mass. He frees her shirt, shaking until it unfurls. The Bell Centre, section 114. During the encore, "Fake Plastic Trees," Josée sat on his lap with her back to Thom Yorke and the rest of the band to make her move. She bit his ear and tugged, then slid her lips across his cheek and onto his mouth, leaving behind a saliva slug trail.

After six months, Josée invited her parents to Sam's apartment for a Thanksgiving dinner.

"It's not Thanksgiving," Sam said.

"Don't care."

Sam wishes he had stayed on no.

Her father repairs audio equipment at Stéreo Vibe, the family business, and her mother does the books. Josée warned, "Dad's a perfectionist, but beneath his strong opinions, he's all kinds of fun." Josée described her mother as angelic. "You don't have to worry about her. She'll love you to bits."

Sam was worried that his apartment was too small to host four people, there wasn't room to turn around.

"Can we eat out?" Sam asked. "Please."

"During a pandemic?" she said. "Are you high? Besides, I have a craving for turkey dinner with all the fixings." She insisted she would take care of all the cooking. She had one more request, "Fix the toilet. It constantly runs." Sam had left a message for Arnold, the building super who posted his name, number and please-call on handwritten notes everywhere. Arnold never answered.

Sam wasn't any good at home repair, so he YouTubed it to discover he needed to replace the fill valve. Pretty straight forward, especially when you watch the step-by-step instructions. Drain the tank, remove the old valve, and put in the new one. Voilà, that constant trickle will be gone. The tank is lined with Styrofoam, and even after the flush, it can be difficult to completely drain. The video suggests a plastic cup to remove most of what remains, and a turkey baster to get into the narrow water-filled crevice around the seal and suck it all up. This prevents water leaking on to the floor when the valve is removed.

Sam replaced the toilet valve the day before the dinner. In his haste, he did not rinse the baster or the beige bits of faded Styrofoam that had collected inside the bulb. Josée used the baster repeatedly, unaware of the Styrofoam being flushed into the gravy and over the turkey.

When they sat down to eat, disaster unfolded.

Her father gnashed a spongy granule on his first bite, "What the hell?"

Pulling it off his tongue, he rolled it between his fingers, like a jeweller examining an uncut gem. He fished others from the gravy and lined the edge of his plate. "What are you feeding us?"

Sam put it all together, right there, and confessed.

Josée was furious. She repeated the same questions, "You used the baster to remove water from the toilet? The toilet?"

Sam kept responding, "No, from the tank. The tank."

He traced a rectangle in the air with two fingers and reacted as though Josée had mistaken beer for champagne.

She called him an idiot, and her father piled on.

"Idiot is too generous. What if I had swallowed that crap?"

Despite her mom's calming efforts—"We all make mistakes, let's enjoy the rest of the meal"—and Sam's repeated apologies, dinner ended, and her parents left. Josée blamed Sam for the humiliation. In the weeks that followed he reached out, but how many times can you ask for forgiveness? His mistake only highlighted all that was wrong with their relationship. Everything had to be examined, held up to the light.

The breakup, paired with COVID, was like an entrée and side dish from hell. It marked the end of Sam's social life. Connecting during a pandemic introduced problems. He tried the dating apps. Where to go? Restaurants and pubs are closed. Going for a walk was common in the warmer months, but in the winter with the windchill coming in at -30 degrees Celsius, forget it. As the virus spread, Sam saw less of other people. For a time, he even saw less of his students as face-to-face classes were replaced with online learning—at least, that's what they called it. They talked about it as though it was real, as though online learning could replace a living, breathing classroom. Zoom and Teams burst onto the scene—non-contact video visitation. The exile was complete.

Right now, Sam flips the Radiohead T-shirt, running his fingers over faded tour dates and stopping on July 17, 2018. He smells it... nothing familiar left. He wants to toss it all in the dryer, but it's tumbling someone else's load.

His pre-pandemic memories seem irreplaceable. One giant domino was pulled from a long line and the forward motion stopped and the world is scrambling to get it going again.

Walking back, he passes Réjean.

"Hey, Sam."

"Rej," Sam nods. "Your load has 20 minutes."

"I know." Réjean's voice trails off down the hall.

"Asshole," Sam says to no one.

Sam's back at his apartment and the lights are out, which is odd. He left them on. He feels the wall for the switch. Can he get the grades in without electricity? *Click*. Kaylee is standing in his kitchen with a frying pan held head high. Her orange hair like a halo of cheese puffs framing a face. She's wearing a navy puffer jacket and the green Hunter boots that belong to her husband. Recognizing Sam, she exhales and lowers the pan to the stove.

"Is he there?"

"Laundry. What's going on?"

She walks to the window and leans on his desk.

"Fire escape?" She points. "Can I make it from your bathroom window?"

"I think so."

She points at the door.

"Lock that."

Sam slides the deadbolt, puts on the chain, and checks the eye hole. Hallway's empty.

She moves into the bathroom, yanking the shower curtain to inspect the window. She slips off her boots leaving them next to the tub. Pulling off her jacket, she drops it, and the zipper clinks off porcelain before landing on the floor. She steps into the tub and swipes a shampoo bottle, conditioner, and bar of soap from the ledge. They fall at her feet. She lifts the latch and slides the frosted window open.

"Fuck, fuck, fuck," she says, "How's this going to work?"

Sam steps over the boots and into the tub, making room between the plastic bottles for his foot, goes down on one knee and slaps it. "Step here."

She does. He puts a hand on her waist, and she puts a hand in his hair, and he's self-conscious about the mess in the bathroom. The grime on the faucet, a wet towel left on the floor. He looks at her pant leg and the ribbed fabric of corduroy, holding his head steady, her fingers press into his scalp. She puts one foot out the window and her touch is gone. The opening is wide enough for her torso to pass. She straddles the frame—sitting half in, half out. Her head rests on the stile, eyes closed.

"Where will you go?" Sam asks.

"My sister's in Lachine. She's waiting. Always waiting. She doesn't know why I stay. I guess I kept telling myself it would get better."

Inch by inch she lowers a foot to a snow free space on the fire escape and takes a couple hops on her socked foot as she pulls out the other leg. Both feet on the ground.

"It can't get any worse."

Sam passes her the boots and jacket through the opening. She snatches them from his hands and slips them on, punching a sleeve hole, she zigzags down the fire escape, while sliding the rest of the jacket on. She rounds the corner in a blur, leaving dark foot holes in the snow. Her breath cloud travels up the building. Sam watches the tiny moisture droplets drift and spread, before closing the window and returning to his desk.

His computer signals an incoming call, and the Teams graphic takes over. His watch reads 8:30 p.m. He clicks the green telephone below the name, Kimberly Meadows.

Her face is unfamiliar.

"Hello, Mr. Anderson. Did you get my email?"

"Uh, no."

"You're muted."

He clicks the microphone on. "No. I didn't read it."

"I'm in your Intro to Psych, Wednesdays and Fridays."

"I know."

Sam takes in her two-dimensional image, her hair held by the clamping jaws of plastic clip. A strand falls over her thick rimmed glasses. She pushes it behind her ear. The glasses, her pallid skin, they give off a level of seriousness paired with desperation. He recognizes her background—

the ceiling, the paint, the window, and the trees. Her room is identical to his.

"Your apartment looks like the Old Orchard."

"I'm on the second floor with my grandparents. I see you on the train, like, all the time."

"I'm late. I mean it's late. What do you want?"

"Can I explain?"

Sam wipes his forehead with the back of his hand and it's damp. "I'm not sure what you can say."

He clears his throat. "To excuse what you did."

"Well."

She sits up straight.

"My grandparents have COVID and they're at Saint Mary's."

Closing her eyes, she leans back in her chair.

"Both are on ventilators."

Her voice breaks on the word ventilators as though she can't breathe.

"I can't visit, no one can."

"I'm sorry."

Sam exhales, leaning forward.

They both look down as though they are staring at the same thing below their computer screens. The same struggle.

"Kim, have you been managing okay?"

"I guess. I don't know. How does anyone ever really know? Schoolwork keeps piling up. I'm so busy with my grandparents. The past three months have been hell. I got desperate."

"Okay, well maybe take a medical leave for the class. If you're caretaker for your grandparents, you qualify. That scrubs it from your transcript. You can retake it in the fall or summer. Contact Catherine Essar."

"I did—I don't qualify. It's too late. Is there anything *you* can do, so we can work this out?"

"We're obligated to report plagiarism, cheating, any of that stuff, and you were performing poorly in my class to begin with, mainly due to your absences."

"Please, sir. Can I redo the paper? My mom is here now. She's staying with me to help. Mr. Anderson, I cannot fail this class."

Sam's tired of having to push back, of enforcing rules he cannot justify in the angry face of a pandemic.

"Okay, listen, take till Monday to resubmit. It's up to you, whether you pass or fail."

"You're being so fair, sir."

Sam ends the call and removes a sweater. It doesn't help. He's boiling. Pain radiates from his head and pounds through his body. It's 9:30. In a marathon session, or maybe it's a final sprint, he grades another fifteen papers, but his focus fades. He keeps reading the same line, from the same paper, again and again and again. He wonders if Kaylee made it to Lachine. What was it like for her, living there, in that pressure cooker?

Wobbly, he stands, walks to the fridge and grabs a lone slice of pizza, tossing the box in the trash. Pepperoni, mushrooms, and green pepper, welded together with cheese, are usually a mouth-watering draw—but he can't eat. He leaves the plated pizza beside some dirty dishes.

At the window, he looks at the maples lining the street below. Snow fills all the branch unions, tracing the reddish-brown bark of every tree branch—mapping hundreds of fractured paths that lead from trunk to crown. The snow finds its way to everything. He opens the window, letting some snow topple into the frame. With his head outside, his breath clouds the air. He listens, but the fresh snow is a giant damper, muting the world.

Then comes the faint rumble of a snow plough leaving Sherbrooke for Old Orchard, pushing the snow into giant heaps. The driver sits alone; the yellow cab light spins out the danger signal. Sam coughs, his stomach tensing so much with each percussion that he can't stop. Pressure mounts behind his eyes. He looks back over his shoulder at his computer. Ten ungraded papers remain and it's 11:50 p.m. There's no way. He leaves the window for his desk, calling up each paper and without reading it, punches in 75/100 for each one.

"Maybe we all need a fucking break."

He continues to the final grade submission screen and hits submit.

Cold dry air blows in through the apartment window, bringing in more flakes. Weak, wanting sleep, Sam slides off his chair to the floor and rolls onto his back. He lays there, still, looking up at the ceiling, pocked and cratered like the surface of the moon. Closing his eyes, he imagines himself in miniature and taking giant steps to cross it. He rolls to his stomach and crawls, looking up at the box spring and mattress. It's too high. On his second attempt he gets on the bed, almost pulling the bedding off and ending up on the floor. His energy spent, he unties and slides his sweatpants down, using a toe to snag and drag the fabric from each leg. The pillowy cotton duvet is like sticky plastic on his skin. The pain spreads, and cuts him into misshapen pieces, fracturing his body from fingertip to chest, like dropped glass. Together, apart. More flakes blow through the window, land and melt, dotting the hard surface of his desk. Coughing, he tries to sleep.

FALLING

PATRICK HEARD the front door close and his father's now classic bumper-car walk. Cracking his bedroom door, he squinted at the man in the dim hallway. And exhaled. Patrick's eyes adjusted to the light. His father bobbed and weaved, as if walking down a moving bridge. His uncertain gait came at $7 a pint.

The father slid his calloused hand across the stovetop for balance, then hit the fridge with his shoulder before his body came to rest in a chair by the kitchen table. The table wobbled, too, if not for the empty match books wedged between the leg and the greasy linoleum.

"Patrick," he bellowed. "My boots. *Patrick!*" He slammed an open hand on the table.

1:00 a.m. If he left the bedroom now, he might miss her, but Patrick knew his father could go on like this for a while. Eyes down, he opened the door and walked toward the kitchen. *Make it quick. No talk—just the boots.*

Patrick bent down and grabbed his father's boot heel. As if on cue, his father, eyes closed, head back, sang an old country tune.

"I'm not through loving you yet—no, I'm not through loving you."

He sounded like a homeless dog.

Patrick knew it was about Mom. When someone close dies, the temperature drops, the leaves fall, and everything else falls with it as gravity sets in like the coming of winter.

Patrick did not know what his father felt and—judging by the amount he drank—it was unlikely his father was capable of feeling it either. When she died, he said it was alcohol or organized religion. "I'll be damned if I'll go to church and listen to all that BS." It was then that Patrick witnessed the alcohol evolution and a preference for country music. It started with brown bottles from local microbreweries, Gastown Amber Ale and Brockton Black Lager. The music was always George Jones, especially "He Stopped Loving Her Today." Then the bottles changed, coming from unfamiliar places that made vodka and rum. Clear bottles with sharp angular edges as though chiseled from granite. Bombora, Cooranbong, Xan, Dragon Bleu, Santiago de Cuba, Angostura, and 10 Cane—but that did not last. That alcohol was too expensive, so Patrick's father made blackberry wine instead. The berries were everywhere, climbing the fence and threatening to overtake the house. A few days of picking and you had enough for a twelve-bottle batch: add a little yeast, monitor the temperature and wait. The large green bottles, fashioned with a metal twist-off lid and a fat neck easy to rinse with the garden hose, littered the floor of the shed.

Every second Friday, Patrick's father took his pay cheque to the neighbourhood pub. Patrick wondered whose neighbourhood, because he didn't recognize anyone in there. The customers stared with eyes easy to read: "Just leave him alone." "Can't you see he's having some fun?" "His wife just died for Christ's sake."

"C'mon, Dad, the mill called, you have an OT shift tomorrow. Finish that one and let's go."

The bartender, leaning over the bright lights of the bar, motioning with his thumb toward the exit like a hitchhiker looking for someone else's ride.

"Get that kid outta here, or I'm gonna lose my license."

At fourteen Patrick couldn't stay for long. He couldn't stay at all.

On those nights, Patrick would have to walk his father home. The walk was slow and meandering, full of ramblings and missed steps, but most of all it was full of a desire to escape the things that had gone wrong for both of them. His father would drape his arm over Patrick's shoulders and trip on the speed bumps meant to slow the cars.

"I love ya, Pat, you know that, don'cha? You're a shootin' star, a shootin' star, and don't let anyone tell you diffr'nt," he would say, squeezing Pat's shoulder. "I may not be the best, but I'm the sec'n from the top, sec'n from the top." Waving two fingers like a peace sign. "Tomorrow, we'll turn this ship around."

Then he would stop and piss in the tall grass. They would continue walking the path leading through the grass field the rest of the way home. Pat had walked the path many times with his father on his way to the grocery store or back from hockey games at the rink. Now, the trail was harder for both of them, and it led to a home they recognized less, all the spaces that had her mark, the kitchen table, her chair at one end, a book, her reading glasses, and a cup of tea—gone. Father and son had to walk there now, with only her memory trapped inside, and when Patrick walked in the front door, he could feel her hand slipping into his. *This was right, little man, what you did for your father.*

His parents' wedding photo, dug up for the funeral, was still enshrined on the mantle. Her short white wedding dress, resting just above the knee, paired with long white gloves that reached her elbow. She held a lavender blue thistle bouquet with a silver baby slipper fastened by ribbon dangling below. His father wore a navy suit and tie, with a white carnation pinned neatly to his lapel. *Click.*

Next to the photo was a wad of greeting cards wrapped tightly with a rubber band. The band was embedded into the furry edges of the cards, frayed from being thumbed too much. The only card not in the pile stood upright and open and belonged to the Heart and Stroke Foundation. *In lieu of flowers, please make a donation to further our research and give back what stroke takes away.* Then there was the turn from this promise to reality, and if you missed it then you fell right off the edge and down into a darkness that had no bottom, because no amount of money would ever bring her back.

Tonight, Patrick's father found his own way home from the pub, and Patrick lifted the dead weight of his father's leg to remove his boot. He pulled, but the boot slid only a few inches then he lost his grip, and Patrick stumbled backward, knocking the kitchen table. *Damn it.* Quickly, he went back to his spot and grabbed hold of the same boot, but it was too late.

Bending his leg to draw Patrick in close—like a fish on a line—his father leaned forward and smacked his right ear. Hard. Patrick, ear ringing, held tight to the boot. Avoiding eye contact, he continued to pull until he removed both boots.

On the way back to his room, Patrick stopped at the fridge, opened the door, reached in and grabbed a bundle of tin foil and shoved it in his pocket. He climbed back in bed with the layers of clothing and blankets heavy on his skin. He wanted off the prison bus.

He heard three gentle fingernail taps from his bedroom window. He jumped up, crossed the room and swept the curtains aside. The front door light revealed a flash of creamy skin against the darkness. There, like a sparkler waving in the dark, streaking to the base of the willow tree. Laura was fearless.

He wedged his fingers into the opening and slid the window ajar. He stood on his toes and hoisted himself up, lifting one leg, then the other, through the open window, and dropped onto the sidewalk below. With the night buzz of crickets in his ears, he took a draw of steamy summer air and jumped over the rhododendron bush. With Laura, a quick embrace, and a whiff of citrus lip gloss. Drawing back, they heard a police siren's wail. The Murphy's dog was next.

The public pool was behind the Murphy's house, so it was quicker to cut through their yard. For the neighbourhood kids the dog existed only in legend. The fence meant they could only *hear* his nightly barking, while the stories about ghastly sharp teeth sprung from their imaginations. Patrick had grabbed the small piece of steak wrapped in tinfoil, just in case. For now, it remained a wet burden oozing into and staining his cargo shorts. Laura and Patrick made their way across the lawn to the side of the house.

Patrick reached through the space between planks on the backyard gate, raised the latch and pushed it open. There, staring back, a playful pit bull terrier well beyond his years. They and the other local kids had wildly overestimated his size and ferocity. Patrick removed the meat from the tinfoil and waved it in the air until Leon's head followed it like a metronome, then he pitched it close to the side wall.

The sound of dog claws on concrete marked Leon's exit when he scrambled toward the juicy castoff. Laura grabbed Patrick's arm, pulling him toward the chain-link fence at the back of the yard. After a short sprint, they reached for the top rail of the fence at the same time, like a pair of synchronized vaulters. At least that was the image Patrick had in mind. But Leon was sharper than he looked, and his teeth presently clamped shut on the bottom of Patrick's cargo shorts. Laura was already over the fence, and their eyes met to the sound of growls and tugs.

"Take them off! Take them off!" Laura said.

He reached for his shorts and wiggled the button free from its hook. With the tension eased, the baggy shorts dropped, and so did Patrick. He kicked both feet bicycle-style as Leon backed away with his prize. Feeling foolish in boxer shorts and sneakers, Patrick stood up and scaled the fence just as the porch light flicked on.

Patrick and Laura continued to run, finally stopping for air under a canopy of cedars.

"You okay?" she gasped.

"I think so," he said, checking his leg for scratches and bite marks. "Fuck, man, that was close. That is the last time we go through the Murphy's."

They laughed, snorting and gasping in unison, then continued to walk 'til they could see the pool. Cool, blue water beckoned. Laura took his hand. Her skin brushed against his forearm; his imagination raced over the rest of her body.

"You sure you want to do this?" asked Patrick.

"Chicken?"

"Okay, relax."

The yellow ball was barely visible, resting in the gutter at the edge of the roof—a discard from the water polo practice earlier in the day. The ball was surrounded by darkness and, if only for a half-inch in either direction, would have remained unnoticed.

Getting onto the changing room roof next to the pool was easy, since city workers covered the hydro metre with a sturdy metal cage. Patrick helped Laura onto the cage, then to grab the edge of the roof, and, before they knew it, they were up looking at the night sky, with the lights of the suburbs glistening like champagne bubbles below.

Standing up there on the roof, they felt safe. Looking down, the pool's hypnotic shimmer reflected their faces as the whir of the filtering system poured into their ears. Up there, no one could touch them.

Laura sat on the incline of the asphalt roof, still warm from the day's sun, and removed her shoes, socks, shorts, underwear and hoodie. This roof was a perfect launching pad.

"Get my bra," she whispered, pointing to her back.

Patrick pinched the clips together with his thumb and forefinger, surprising them both with his tactful removal. She quickly snatched it, rolled everything up into a ball and pitched it to the pool deck below. He could just make out her naked silhouette with the light from the pool. He wanted her to stand still a moment more, so he could curl up in her arms and be carried off into the night sky.

His gaze turned reluctantly to the sloping roof. The speed needed to reach the water, and the uncertainty of exactly where the roof ended and nothingness began, combined to create a small-town rite of passage.

"Me first," he said stepping out of his boxers and bending an elbow to remove his T-shirt.

Carefully pushing her hair behind her ear, she leaned over and gently kissed him. Her lips felt soft and moist, like the flesh of an orange. Then he was off. Standing at the apex of the roof, Laura watched as he took several quick steps and jumped. He was airborne, with toes pointed and arms tight to his sides. The cool air lifted his hair up and over his head, and for a moment he seemed pinned to the air. The light from the pool illuminated his skin as he punctured the water and sank, right down to the bottom. Bobbing back to the surface, he made his way over to the ladder at the side of the pool eager to watch her glorious descent from the rooftop.

"Nice jump, Pencil Boy. How's the water?" she asked.

"Perfecto."

"Wait a sec. I'll be in soon."

He watched her lean over, take a deep breath, and make a break for the water. The squeak from the ball when her foot hit, was almost imperceptible, but it was there, and distinctly out of place compared to the other sounds that reached his ears. He heard nails on a chalkboard. The ball compressed and wedged deeper into the gutter, while Laura's fall carried her straight down and to the left of the open water. She dropped through the air all twisted and tangled, like she was wrapped in a parachute. For a moment, she was lost to the darkness. Then, spat back out, her body slapped the concrete. Just below the lifeguard chair. No scream, no call for help. She just dropped—a lifeless, naked discard from the sky. Dark rivulets spread over the concrete from her hair to form a larger pool, like the continent of some strange new world.

When the headlights rolled down the blinds of the police station, Patrick knew his father had pulled up. Patrick stood and looked at the policeman working the front counter.

The cop nodded toward the door, "I suggest you find some pants."

Patrick opened the door, ran down the steps, and bolted right past his father. He crossed the street—running flat out on the King George Highway. Past the Milk Jug, Chevron, and Jo Anne's Hair Salon. He crossed the street after passing a large flashing neon sign. *Save the heat, install new doors and windows now*! He followed the concrete sidewalk for two or three kilometers all the way up to 104th Avenue. Out of breath, he could see the Memorial Hospital parking lot and the front entrance.

His mom's night shift would have normally ended soon, and she would have been preparing for the drive home. If only they could talk one more time. She would help him figure this all out.

Patrick made his way to the main entrance, careful not to trigger the automatic sliding doors, and looked inside. He expected to see his mom's elbows resting on the laminate counter, tightly pinned auburn hair, pressed white uniform, embroidered white cross on a navy-blue background below her left shoulder, pen in hand, documenting the interruptions in other people's lives. Instead, there was an empty nursing station, and him in boxers and running shoes staring in, his breath fogging up the glass.

She wouldn't say, "What the hell were you thinking? What the hell were you doing up there in the middle of the night anyway?" She would listen. Carefully digesting the words as they spilled from his lips. Then she would pose these precise questions *right here* and *right there*. In the end, everyone would be standing together, face to face with the uncertainty of it all. "With each second a new series of events unfolds that brings many possibilities. The truth is we don't know what will happen next, Pat. I can tell you this: You can't live a real life, I mean, you can't really experience all that life has to offer, if you are constantly afraid of what might happen next."

Footsteps. A reflection in the glass. The crunchy *swish* of the sliding glass door. A hand on his shoulder.

"Look," his father said, "I know you're pissed at me. I spoke to admissions and she's waking up now and asking for you. They think she has a good chance.

"Now put these on," he said, handing him a pair of sweatpants. "*Jesus.* Where are your clothes?"

Patrick slid on the sweatpants his father gave him.

"Look, we follow the blue line to the ICU and bed seven. You know your way around this place."

As they walked into the hospital the morning sun followed, casting its light through the gaps, little openings that allow some light to shine through—so we can find our way.

WAYS TO HOLD A GUN

Mark is Delilah Letestu's third grade teacher. He exhales slowly, ballooning his cheeks, before dialing her father again. "Get lost!" *Click*. Does Mr. Letestu think it's someone selling something?

Mark punches in the number.

This time, Mr. Letestu says, "Hello?" And waits.

"Hi, uh... this is Mark Sutter, Delilah's teacher."

"I know who you are."

"We're sending her home."

"Go ahead. I'll bring her right back."

"She was caught stealing."

"Stealing what?"

"Better if we talk in person."

"You fucking people. I'll be there in forty-five."

Click.

When Mark crosses the reading carpet, he steps over Earth and the rest of the solar system, but after talking with Mr. Letestu, he feels small. He wonders what he could have said.

He takes Delilah's behaviour report and a set of ungraded spelling tests into the hall, stopping in front of a bulletin board of artwork. Chalk drawings on black construction paper: twenty-two polar bears stare back at him. The kids were given the same instructions, so each one has an upside-down triangle for a nose, jellybean eyes, and back-to-back fishhooks for a mouth. But each bear is different. One has pointy ears, another a square head, one is not completely coloured in. Mark feels like the polar bear.

Two weeks before the start of school, he moved from Vancouver to Las Vegas. All those Clark County ads citing a teacher shortage—and the sunny Southwest itself—brought him here. He loved the rain because, in Vancouver, you had to. But after the death of his mother there was nothing and no one to keep him. She had also taught elementary. Growing up, she surrounded him with books, and all that information helped him make sense of most things. Except his father. As Mark got older, he asked more questions, but it was a conversation she didn't like to have. Maybe it was Mark's mannerisms, the way he crossed his fork and knife when he'd finished his plate. "I never taught you that." She told him the relationship was brief. His name was Kelly and he was a card player from Reno. Mark picked that up, too. There was joy in cards, whether it was poker or blackjack. It could bring people together, and drive them apart. Maybe the cards brought him hope that one day they'd meet.

Mark never forgot his mom's advice to get a teaching degree, so he could go anywhere in the world: Japan, South Korea, the States. "But while you're young go somewhere warm, sweetheart," she said, "someplace you can hang a towel to dry, and it doesn't stay damp and musty. And remember, you care for those kids, all of them, the good, the bad, and the ugly, as if they were yours."

After she died, Mark completed his degree, quit his job as shipper-receiver at Lumberland and applied for a dozen teaching positions in the Southwest. Three months later, he got the job in Vegas. They wouldn't cover his moving expenses; he had to get there on his own. With his cat Mylo in a carrier on the passenger seat of his Civic, a guitar and two suitcases in the trunk, he took the I-5 to Seattle, then southeast past Boise, and when he hit Twin Falls it was a straight shot to the desert. Still miles from Vegas, on the edge of the Mojave, he spotted an island of buildings and, shooting up from it, the Luxor Sky Beam. His first look at the Las Vegas Strip, and he felt the draw: a need to be closer to lights, gambling, and audacity.

Mark continues down the hall to the atrium and sits in the open—no corners to get backed into—and he waits for Mr. Letestu. Plate glass windows let the light in. It's January, and the real heat doesn't start until June. Felix, the security guard, mans a desk at the command post in the centre of the atrium. He notices Mark sitting below the school's name and logo: *Spring Mountain Elementary—Where We Climb Mountains Every Day!*

"Mornin', Mr. Sutter."

White noise comes from his radio. Felix eyes his belt, pinching the dial to lower the volume.

"Mornin', Felix."

"I hear we might have a visitor."

"Just confirmed. He'll be here in forty-five minutes."

"I've got the footage cued, say the word."

The faculty knows Jerome Letestu. He has four kids, and Delilah's the youngest. Some teachers have fared better than others with the Letestus, but even Mrs. Augustine, a twenty-year veteran, went on sick leave because of Jerome.

In Vegas, people carry handguns loaded and ready in their cars. Jerome preferred his in a hip holster. Before the legislation banning open carry in public buildings, he wore it to his son's suspension meeting at Spring Mountain. That was a problem for Mrs. Augustine. She asked Jerome if he could place it in his car, told him it made her uncomfortable. He said, "No way. They'll need to rewrite the constitution first." The vice principal asked him to leave the premises. Jerome did leave but returned the following day with his gun by his side. Police were called, but there was little they could do: "Sorry, ma'am, it's state law." It made the papers: *Clark County School District Sued for Banning Gun-Carrying Parent*. Jerome was quoted in the article.

"What price does a jury put on being humiliated in front of your children for exercising your constitutional rights?"

Mark hears gun talk everywhere. It puts him on edge, changes the way he drives. Never honk, gesture, or make eye contact with other drivers. Soon after he arrived in Vegas, he watched a twenty-minute news broadcast from his apartment, *When Is It Okay to Shoot a Trespasser?* Mark thought never; he was wrong. According to the stand-your-ground-laws, if a trespasser is threatening to kill or harm someone, then deadly force can be used.

Mr Soros, a fourth-grade teacher at Spring Mountain, teaches in the classroom beside Mark and owns a .357 Magnum. "You want to see it?" he had asked. Mark followed him to the parking lot, not sure what to expect. It was recess, the kids were on the jungle gym fifty metres away. Mark sat in the passenger seat while Mr. Soros dropped the glovebox door. He slid out a brushed aluminum case and placed it on Mark's lap. Mark popped the latch; the gun was nesting in purple velour, like a royal sceptre. He eyed the long barrel, and the finger grooves fluting the criss-crossed rubber-coated grip.

"What's this?" he pointed at a red stopper.

"Trigger block."

Mark picked up the gun by the barrel between his finger and thumb, then held it with both hands, palms up like he was reading a book. Mark didn't know how to hold it, if he wasn't going to shoot.

"That's something," Mr. Soros said, "ain't it?"

"Will it make the bad men run?"

"Four people in my family were shot, including me: three cousins and an uncle. Gang related, debts to be paid, scores to be settled... I guess."

He rolls up his sleeve to show Mark a bicep bullet wound. It looks like a fat piece of gum ironed into his skin.

"That's not a birthmark. I'm at a traffic light and two guys get out of the car ahead of me. I saw the gun right away. One put a shot through the driver's side window as I backed up. Intimidation is their best weapon, and other times they shoot."

Ms. Lee, the vice-principal, pulls up a chair next to Mark. She is petite, with red frame glasses and a tan pantsuit, her black hair in a bob. She pushes it aside like a stage curtain, opening to highlight her face. She smiles.

"I spoke to Delilah at the office. She has her schoolbag, homework, and lunch. I told her to remain there until she is invited over. Did you make the call?"

"Just got off the phone. He's upset, and on his way. Any advice?"

"Jerome's a handful. He'll convince you he's calling in the National Guard. He's going to be angry. Expect it. You're in a position of authority."

"What should I do?"

"It'll be tough, till you establish some trust. Build a relationship. You haven't had a chance to, so today, let him talk. Be professional. When you have the opportunity to speak, take it. Tell him that her suspension is part of a necessary, predetermined sequence of events. Give him the itemized behaviour report."

"I made a copy."

"Give him the original."

The report lists eighteen infractions over three months, with the date and a brief note for each. *Crawling under a locked bathroom stall when other children are using it*; *writing "ass-face" on her neighbour's desk with permanent marker; tearing a handful of hair from an opponent's head during a game of soccer.* Mark was reluctant to call home for any of it. If he did, his classroom management would be called into question. Two teachers had already been fired from the school. This morning, Felix provided CCTV footage of Delilah rummaging through Josiah's backpack and pocketing his book fair money. Word got out to the higher-ups.

"Okay, good," says Ms. Lee, reviewing the report. "Do you have the school code of conduct?"

He nodded.

"Perfect. You're ready. I'll take your class to the cafeteria when they return from music."

"She went too far," Mark says.

"Yep. When I started here, the principal at the time pulled me aside and said, 'You need to lay into these kids, let 'em have it. Yell, point a finger, whatever it takes—make them feel your disappointment. Be over the top, or they won't think you care.'"

Ms. Lee stands, spins, and walks toward the music room.

Mark turns to his spelling tests, correcting one word at a time, convinced he can do the same with his students. But what if he's wrong? What if he can't? On the first paper, he crosses out a lowercase *j* and writes a capital *J* for the word *January;* he places an X. The second word is *trader*, but the student has written *traitor*. Mark places an X and writes: *spelled correctly but wrong word*.

He stops grading, stands and looks across the atrium and through the glass wall at the office. Delilah sits, swinging her feet back and forth. He turns to the front of the school, void of children and grass, a field of crushed river rock. Three-barrel cacti are planted beside a flagstone walkway; the knee-high cacti are covered in yellow spines.

Mark looks at Felix, still sitting at his post. "Any kids ever run into them, the cactus?"

"Never. Kids don't play out there. But if you do, white glue—cover your skin, let it dry, and pull it off. Most of the spines go along with it, especially the small ones."

Mark sees Jerome approach the school entrance and press the intercom.

Felix speaks into the mic. "Yes?"

"Jerome Letestu. Here to see Mr. Sutter."

"Come in."

Felix nods at Mark. "Showtime."

Jerome, dressed in a navy Adidas tracksuit and yellow neon Nike's, crosses the carpeted floor. With a flick of his tongue, a toothpick travels from mouth corner to mouth corner. He slides out a chair from under a circular table, removes his track jacket and drapes it over the back. His triceps bulge as he lowers into the chair across from Mark.

"Ya know, I should call the paper and tell them what goes on in here," he says. "Tell them how our tax money is spent. You think it's fine, don'tcha?"

He removes the toothpick from his mouth and rolls it between his finger and thumb, pointing it in time with his words.

"You think you know what you're doing when it comes to teaching my kid? You're wrong."

Jerome's voice fills the atrium. Felix moves closer.

Mark places his hands on the table and uses them to pull himself forward in his chair. His hands leave sweat prints on the tabletop. "Look, Mr. Letestu, I get it, you're frustrated."

"'I get it, you're frustrated?'" Jerome repeats, titling his head to the side. "Is that what they teach you to say to angry parents? You got kids of your own, Sutter?"

"No, sir."

"You want the world for them and will do whatever it takes to give 'em a fair shot."

"Yes, sir, exactly—so let's get back to Delilah. This morning, I asked the class to hand in their book fair money and order forms, and Josiah said his money was in his backpack, but now it's gone."

"So, how'd you know Delilah took it?"

"Felix has CCTV footage of her in the hall, rummaging through his bag. We can show it to you. I confronted her, and she pulled the money from her desk. And this is not the first time her behaviour has been challenging."

Mark hands him the behaviour report.

Jerome snatches the paper. "What's this?"

"It lists Delilah's behaviour in the past three months."

As Jerome reads, he inhales slowly and lifts his eyebrows.

"Why'd you wait so long to show me this?"

"Until today, the problems weren't serious, but theft is an automatic two-day suspension."

Mark slides a planner across the table and opens it to the school code of conduct. "I've highlighted it"—he points to the centre of the page—"here and here."

Jerome turns in his chair to face the office.

"Delilah Justice Letestu!"

He waves an arm to catch her attention.

"Get out here!"

The secretary nods and Delilah leaves the office, head down, dressed in her school uniform: a maroon polo shirt, with navy knit socks and skirt. Her eyes are brick brown and moist, but she's not crying. Her hair is wound into a bun on the top of her head. She lifts her chin as she walks up to Jerome, stands beside him, and eyes her teacher.

"Yes, sir."

"Is it true? Did you steal this money?"

"Yes, sir."

"What in the hell are you doing taking someone else's money, girl? You know better. Goddamnit!" He strikes the table with the palm of his hand. "I raised you better."

Delilah looks down at her feet. "I know."

"Get back there!" He points at the office. "Until we're ready to leave."

"Yes, sir."

Delilah turns, walks to the office and slumps into her chair.

Shaking his head, Jerome stands.

"She'll be back in two days."

He lifts his jacket and slips it on.

"You won't have no more trouble. And get those kids on the goddamn computer!"

After work, Mark drives to the strip and parks at Planet Hollywood. They have a daily no-limit hold 'em poker tournament. Mark wants in. He passes the Pleasure Pit, walks up to the cashier and drops his money in the drawer. "Ones, fives and quarters, please." He collects the chips and scratches at a 3-D image of Elvis with his thumbnail, lifting some of the plastic laminate. He spots a table with two players. He recognizes one of them from the day before. Same backward Bass Pro Shops ball cap, same mirrored glasses.

"I figured after what happened yesterday," she says, "you wouldn't be back."

"Looks like you never left."

"Touché."

Marks rubs his hands together—"Let's play some cards!"—and nods at the dealer.

When Delilah returns from her suspension, Mark books the computer lab three times a week, dropping his free period to teach the kids typing, word processing and how to create a spreadsheet. He has the kids put their skills to work by creating the Spring Mountain Stock Exchange. "You will each be given 100 Sutter Bucks to invest in the company of your choice." The bills are photocopied cutouts with images of his grinning face. They come in $5, $10, and $20 denominations. *In Sutter We Trust*. The kids are crazy for it. In teams of four, they create a company name, slogan and marketing strategy for class presentations. "Remember the goal here, people. You want your classmates to invest in your company. You want them to buy into your way of thinking."

Delilah and her team design a private school called Jackpot Special that has horse stables, an amusement park, and a shooting range.

Mark wheels up a chair next to the team's computer and reviews the aerial map they created on *Minecraft*.

"Bird's-eye view. Nice."

Delilah zigzags the cursor across the screen, then hovers over the stable.

"You can ride your horse on a hundred acres," she says, "and you could even use your horse to get to class. Did you see the roller coaster over here?"

"A shooting range?" Mark asks, pointing to an area on the map with targets, rifles, and handguns. "How did you make those guns?"

"You can make a handgun, sniper rifle, or a machine gun with iron ingots and red stone dust. You need the command block and a texture pack."

She squints one eye and leans back from the screen to look at him. "Don't you know nothin'?"

"Delilah...."

"What are you 'fraid of?"

"Who's afraid? I'm curious about your project."

"People will be linin' up to go to our school. My Dad could teach gun class, ya know, make sure everyone knows how to hold it. How to check if it's loaded."

She closes one eye and points her finger gun, lowering it to line it up with the computer screen. "Aim."

"And fire!"

Bending her thumb trigger. "*Bang! Bang! Bang!* He could even show you, Mr. Sutter. If you want. Everyone should know how to fire a gun."

"Invite your Dad to class. He can give the gun talk."

"Really?"

"He's going to teach at your school, isn't he? Your Dad, working for you, eh, Delilah?"

Mark pushes her shoulder.

"Good job."

Delilah stares at Mark, mouth open, eyes wide.

The class is on the reading carpet watching Jerome tack up gun photos: rifles, AK-47s and Glocks, using circular magnets to fix them to the board.

"These are the weapons for the firing range. We can keep 'em, and we can bear 'em. Remember, kids, the US government ain't afraid to trust us with arms."

Jackpot Special secures the most investors. It's like the chance to make more money is real, the guns are real, and all the kids want in. It kindles a dream. But Mark wonders what kind of dream?

"All right, everyone," he says. "All the companies have gone public, and you have secured investors. Trading will begin at the end of next week, when the Spring Mountain Stock Exchange officially opens."

At the end of the day, Delilah brings her planner to Mark's desk. He reads a note inside.

Come for dinner. Bring whatever you like. I wanna talk cards.

Jerome

Mark has been spending a lot of time gambling in the casinos. It hasn't been easy meeting people or making friends or having a meal in someone's home. His guitar case sits in the corner of the class, unopened. He reads the message again, and with the ending, *I wanna talk cards,* comes a shot of panic.

Mark has continued to play, but he had a system, a limit; an amount in his mind. And once he hit it, he would stop. He followed this rule carefully, until last week. With one good hand and too much confidence, he bet the pot.

And lost. Mark owes the house $14,000.00. He doesn't have the money. Yet.

Delilah lingers.

"So?" She smiles. "Can you come?"

"Sure. What should I bring?"

"Chocolate cake."

The next day, Mark gathers his things and heads out to the car. Exiting the building in the dark, he hears the radio buzz of the cicadas—at night, the desert is alive. He pulls out of the lot and onto Martin Luther King Boulevard. Gravel is everywhere grass should be. The light standards arch over the road like the ribs of some gigantic animal, and a constant wind blows, sandblasting all the exposed metal. The asphalt is tinged brown, covered in sand like it was spread on with an icing knife, a reminder the desert wants back what it lost.

All the houses are beige stucco, stamped out identical. He presses hard on the gas, and they flap by like the pages in a flipbook. There are no gated communities in North Las Vegas, not like Summerlin or Henderson. No pool in every yard. No pass code for the main gate; no full-time, armed security guard screening every entrant. Anyone can drive in or out. Isn't that the way it should be? No drip systems soaking the ground three times a day for seven minutes each to maintain the green. Each house is exposed on all sides, and the dry earth crumbles. All the homes have bars over the ground level windows, and most have a wrought iron screen door at the entrance. Everywhere the message: protect yourself.

Mark arrives at Cheyenne Drive, pulls in next to an 84 Escalade and slides the shifter into park. He feels like backing out and driving the twelve hundred miles home to Vancouver, but he turns off the ignition, opens the door with one hand and slides the other under the chocolate cake in the front seat, careful not to upset the Saran Wrap elevated by toothpicks to protect the icing. He inches his way out, lets the door close on its own, unable to lock it, he walks up to the front of the house. He feels like the warm-up comic at one of those Cirque du Soleil shows down on the strip. The one sent out to get the audience laughing, before the real show starts. He presses the bell.

The front door opens, and Delilah is there in a purple dress. She turns the deadbolt on the screen door, and Mark pulls it open.

"Mr. Sutter is here!"

Mark enters the foyer.

"All right," Jerome says, stepping into the light, "take the cake, invite our guest into the living room, and ask if he would like a drink."

"I'll take a Coke," Mark says, "if you have one."

"Go on, Delilah, put the cake on the kitchen counter, wash your hands, and pour drinks for all of us."

"Yes, Dad."

With both hands under the cake, Delilah walks into the kitchen.

Mark reaches into his front pocket, presses the fob to lock the car, and listens for the chirp.

Jerome shakes Mark's hand and pulls him close, hissing, "You know why you're here, Sutter? I'm at the Nugget. I work outta the backroom. It's Monday morning, and you can imagine my surprise when I see your fucking name on the board! My daughter's teacher?" He screws his face up. "Your address. Your employer. Your phone number. You owe fourteen large. Fourteen large? You gotta get your name off that board. They're comin'. They start with the door of your house. For real. They tear it off, hinges and all, and the whole world can see you, sittin' at your kitchen table in your goddamn underwear, eatin' your cornflakes. It'll get back to Spring Mountain. Bet on it. And Delilah's having her best school year. You got her talking 'bout college. It might be her ticket out. I'm tryin' to help. You didn't come all the way to Vegas to lose. Did you?"

"I blew it. I need more time."

"We all need more time. You got the money?"

"I'm working on it. Waiting on the credit check. I'll have it."

"You better."

Delilah walks in with three glasses of Coke carefully balanced on a TV tray, the ice cubes at the top of each glass tinkling her arrival. Her eyes are locked on to the drinks, as if her stare can prevent a spill.

The next morning, Mark slips out the door of his apartment. "No, no buddy." Hopping on one leg, he uses his other foot to block Mylo's escape. He closes the door. "I want you inside today."

He locks it. Mylo jumps between the curtain and windowpane, with his paw punching at the glass.

Mark surveys the parking lot, and a drop of perspiration trickles down his rib cage. *Bank of America, 3:30.* He drives to school. In class, he rearranges the magnetized signs on the board, so "Mad Math Minute" is followed by "Class Meeting" and "Journal Time!" He pushes all the chairs under the desks and lays out a math sheet. He picks up the whiteboard marker, removes the cap and turns the marker so the long edge of the chiseled tip lays flat against the board. He writes the date and a journal starter phrase: *If I could change one thing about today, I would....*

He leaves the classroom and walks to the back of the school, where the kids line up. They see him approach. Delilah's at the front, clutching her backpack with both arms like a bulging grocery sack. She stares at him. The backpack slips, she boosts it up and squeezes, but her cellphone drops. The corner of the phone strikes the concrete. The phone spins and comes to rest face down. No one wants to pick it up to see the damage. Mark does, and there is a crack across the screen. He lightly runs his finger along it, but the sharp edge cuts him anyway.

Blood beads from a tiny hole.

He puts his finger in his mouth.

He slides the phone into his pocket.

The kids see it all, the talking stops, and with furrowed brows they stare at Mark, as if to say: *Someone's in big trouble now.*

"I'm sorry," Delilah says, "it slipped."

"You know you shouldn't have a phone at school. You'll get it back at the end of the day. To take home."

"Are you okay?"

"I'm fine. All right, people, let's get this day started, we've got work to do."

With Mark at the head of the line, they snake through the school to their class. The students hang their jackets in the hall and put on indoor shoes. Always in transition, always moving from one thing to the next, each moment planned.

"All right, folks, bring me those planners."

The fire alarm sounds.

"Okay, everyone lineup at the door. You know the drill, we've practised this: we go to the parking lot. Quietly. Makayla, you're last, so lights out, door closed."

The bell continues to ring, even though all hundred and eighty-three students are now in the playground next to the school parking lot, arranged in long lines, facing teachers with clipboards who check off their names. So few, responsible for so many. *Is everyone here?* The winding cry of a fire truck moves closer to the school.

Felix walks by, brings a hand to his mouth and whispers to Mark, "This was not planned, someone pulled it."

Mark surveys the school building, looking for smoke, and sees a plastic bag, miles up in the air, twisting and turning as it mounts the sky.

A student asks, "What happened to your car, Mr. Sutter?"

"My car?"

Mark spins to face the lot.

His car is two rows back from where all the kids have lined up, and the driver's door is missing. You can see the black cloth interior, his coffee mug in the cup holder, and a gym bag on the passenger seat. It's like the car was in a demolition derby.

"Shit," Mark mutters, but to the students he says, "All right, all right. Let's not worry about that."

A fire truck arrives. Two men jump out in full gear, wearing masks and Scott Air-Paks. Moments later, they exit the school alongside Ms. Lee, who speaks into a bullhorn.

"Okay, Spring Mountain, I need your attention. Nice work evacuating! We have the all-clear. It's safe to return to class. Your attention goes to your teacher."

When everyone has returned, Mark sits at his desk. Delilah approaches him.

He tells the class, “Planners out and ready.”

“I want you to have this, Mr. Sutter,” Delilah whispers, shoving her backpack forward.

“You’ve been carrying it all morning. What’s in it? I don’t like surprises.”

“Look,” she says with a nod, “inside. Beside my lunch.”

Mark unzips the first pocket and sees a gun muzzle poking up between her lunch and planner. He tries to swallow. He can’t. His mouth is too dry. He squeezes the bag shut, careful not to let anyone see what he saw.

“Why do you have this?” he whispers.

Delilah stares in a way that suggests he should know.

And the fear that started at his apartment swells and bangs his brain. He looks around the room, then goes back to the bag, and pulls her lunch and planner from the bag.

“Take these to the cloakroom in the hall. Wait for me there.”

“But Mr. Sutter—”

“Now, Delilah.”

She leaves.

With the gun inside, he zips up the backpack and places it in his deep drawer. He goes to the front of the class, masking fear with a poker face.

"All right, everyone, calm down, we've all had a busy morning."

He waits for the last voice to die out.

"But you guys can handle this. You can handle anything. Shawn, I want you to collect all the planners and place them opened and face down on my desk. The rest of you, time for the Mad Math Minute. Now, listen up, when you finish, I want you to put on your artist's hat. Draw the firemen and the truck on the back of your sheet. Let's see who can draw the best truck, hose, and ladder—remember, I want detail. Fill in the white space. Does everyone understand?"

"Yes, Mr. Sutter," comes the echo.

"Go!"

He places the egg timer on the whiteboard tray, and the students flip their papers, heads held low.

Mark walks into the hall cloakroom. It's empty except for Delilah.

"Does your dad know about this?"

"He told me to bring it."

"For me?"

She nods.

"Did you tell anyone?"

"Nope."

"Okay, we're not going to talk about this. Understood?"

"Yes, sir."

"You could get into major trouble for this. Major."

"But you need it for protection. It's okay to be scared."

"I don't, I mean I'm not." He points to the class with his thumb. "Now get back in there."

Delilah enters the class, but Mark stays behind, closing his eyes and focusing on his breathing. His diaphragm goes down and in, and his chest lifts. He wonders if he can really fix this. What about his car with no door? Can he drive it? He needs that credit approval, that cash—today. *Jesus.*

He stops at the fountain in the hall to gulp down some water then wipes his lips with the back of a hand. He pulls his phone from his pocket and dials Jerome's number.

"Are you outta your mind?"

There's silence, the sort that suggests someone is listening.

In a whisper, Jerome says, "You put it in your bag. Keep it with you. They know your schedule. Don't follow it. Leave early. To be safe, you run the lights at Flamingo and Jones, that's where they get someone to jump in the car. If not, they'll tail you."

Click.

Walking back into his room, Mark notices the egg timer has run out. Some of the kids are drawing now, pulling out pencil crayon packs and laying them flat on their desks.

"Once you finish the drawing, start your journal. Mrs. Curtis will be visiting, so make it good."

Mark slides out the deep desk drawer then closes it. He checks his watch. How did he get here? He opens the drawer again, pulls out the backpack and feels the dead weight of the gun. He wants it out of the classroom, away from the children. He imagines pulling it from the bag and hurling it into the desert. A spray of sand kicks up where it lands. Harmless, no one near it, half-buried and baking in the sun. Over time, the gunmetal loses its blue lustre and windblown grains of sand get into the barrel, the cylinder, and the moisture leads to corrosion, locking all the moving parts. A gun made meaningless—no longer a way out, or a way in.

He calls the office secretary.

"Could you send Mrs. Curtis to cover me?"

When she arrives, Mark shoulders the backpack.

"It's *Journal Time!* Mrs. Curtis, could you please circulate and check their entries? I'm stepping out until lunch."

He gives Felix a nod and exits the back of the school. *Get to the bank.* He speeds up his pace. *Get the money. Get to the Casino.* The parking lot is quiet, the usual cars. The morning sun casts long shadows. He pulls out his keys, and they tangle in the key ring. He shakes them free, but they drop. *Fuck. Fuck.* He picks them up and looks through the rear door window to check the back seat. All clear. He gets in, then reaches for the door, from the habit of having to close one—but it's gone. He places the backpack on the passenger seat beside his gym bag.

"Mr. Sutter!" Felix waves at him from the school building. "Sunglasses, you left them in the staff room."

Mark runs over. "Thanks, probably need these."

"You better get that door fixed."

"Top of my list." Mark notices the security officer's badge on his chest pocket; the brass finish, an insignia with the words *protective force* encircling a map of the world.

"Hey, Felix."

"Yes?"

"Enjoy the rest of your day."

"Will do boss."

Mark puts his sunglasses on, walks back to his car, and settles into the driver's seat. He turns the key. The staccato of the ignition is quiet. *tick—tick—tick.* He tries again, and as the battery voltage drops it slows, *tick——tick,* but the car catches. He releases the steering wheel and leans back into his seat, staring up at the atrium roof, then beyond at the peak of La Madre. The desert spreads out around that mountain, bruised with shadows of Joshua Trees, twisted and bristled, but none are in bloom.

He reaches back into the bag to check for the gun, but it's not there. He sits up, places the bag on his lap, unzips it further, and rummages through the tidal pool of pencils and erasers, trying not to panic.

The recess bell sounds; it's a crescendo of three notes. *Ding-Ding-Ding.* The school doors burst, ricocheting off doorstops, and the kids are out, running and laughing.

Mark sees a man's face in the rear-view. He's sitting in the back seat. Pale skin, and high cheekbones that protrude from the hoodie. Mark turns to face him. The man glances at the kids on the playground and ducks. Through the seat, Mark feels the barrel in his back.

"Looking for this? Cowboy? Drive," the man hisses, "just fucking drive."

Mark rests his forehead on the steering wheel, closes his eyes, and turns off the engine. "I'm not going anywhere."

THE WEIGHT OF SOMEONE ELSE

STONES CHURN UP every year, tectonic debris from some deep place. Kneeling, Cooper Reynolds pulls one up: it's dark, angular. He turns the stone in his hand and squeezes to be sure it's not just a hard chunk of dirt he can crumble back to the garden. "You son of a bitch," he says, pitching it into the woods. A *crunch* comes from the dead leaves. "After all those miles, *that's* your final destination." The jackhammer-like sound of a jake brake drifts in from the neighbouring highway, reminding Cooper of Peg. She would have turned sixty-five today.

Cooper is sturdy and lean, arms corded—a body of labour.

"Jack of all, master of none," he likes to say. Most of his life, he's worked construction. The pleasure comes from the lift, carry, and push. With each stride his heart rate climbs: *Lub dub, Lub dub*. The vigour spills out, leaving behind the things he builds and some he helps destroy.

Watching him in the garden you'd think he could go forever, but he's seventy. And last week, mowing the lawn, his heart stuck at 150 beats per minute—a constant rev in the motor. A beat that refused to slow, even after Cooper reclined in the La-Z-Boy with a glass of ice water to read the *Vancouver Sun*. He dialed 9-1-1. *We-you, We-you*, the ambulance took him to Emergency.

A triage nurse took his information and put him in a small examination room.

"The cardiologist will be in to see you shortly," she said.

Cooper heard the doctor pull the manila folder from the door pouch and the *snap* of flipped pages. Why was the folder kept outside? To protect him from himself?

Cooper hates hospitals. Everyone else knows what you don't.

Keeping her eyes on the folder, the doctor entered the room, "Hello Mr. Reynolds," she said. "So, I'm seeing atrial fib. You can stop it with electric shock or medication. The zap is more aggressive, but the medication works too."

Cooper went with the zap, and his heart returned to a regular rhythm. Cooper's body, for so long a thing he could trust, is beginning to fail.

He yanks the pull cord on the tiller, and a couple hollow chugs are followed by a loud steady flutter of the two-stroke engine. With all that noise, Cooper expects lift off. He releases the clutch and black soil cascades from a Ferris wheel of blades. In rubber boots, Cooper sinks deep and moves slow, holding the tiller back so it doesn't get ahead of him, each furrow marked with a boot print. After his last pass, he cuts the engine, lifts a ball cap from silvery hair, and wipes the sweat with the crook of his arm. He slips his cap back on, pivots the tiller, freeing the blades, and wheels it to the woodpile. The grey plywood piece he uses to cover the tiller is thin and warped, so he centres a boulder on top to hold it there. He rubs his back before straightening up. Buckled and bent are now regular positions, as if aging meant a return to the foetal position.

Cooper hears a car door and turns to see his eldest, Steve, in a navy suit and tie, standing beside an Audi, jingling keys. He knows Steve wants that tiller to zip around the neighbourhood and plough it all under to make room for bigger homes on smaller lots, with swimming pools and hot tubs, new trees, shrubs and lawns like carpet. Then he'd have them put in a network of footpaths and concrete sidewalks with painted lines and crosswalks at all of the intersections. Some of the paths would lead to a park, just big enough for people to gather and chat while their dogs take a crap. When he's done, what'd be left is a new subdivision with a high walkability score.

"Dad, how are you?"

"One foot in the grave, the other on a banana peel."

"Shouldn't you wear ear protection?"

"What?"

He smiles, walking past Steve to the willow. He disappears behind some switches like he's moving behind a stage curtain. He goes for the trunk of the willow and grabs a shovel leaning nearby, reappears and says, "I've a garden to plant—especially the potatoes. Remember, when I'd get you to weed an entire row of carrots for a dollar in quarters, and you'd go to the arcade."

"Ya well, it's the first week of April. A bit early, isn't it?"

"Early?" Cooper repeats. "Feel that heat and know this—every year it comes sooner."

He moves to a corner of the garden. "What do you know anyway? Real farmers don't look at the calendar."

Stepping on the blade, Cooper drives the shovel in and wiggles the handle to loosen the soil and lift out a scoop.

"You're not a *real* farmer," Steve says. "You have a vegetable garden."

"I farm, therefore I am."

Cooper tosses a shovel of soil into the center of the garden. *Thud.*

"The world has about sixty years of topsoil left. Can you believe it? We're eroding the earth's fragile skin."

"Alright, Old MacDonald, can we talk? I'm on lunch."

Cooper knows that Steve worries about his father's finances. He wants to see preparation. When Peg died without a will, no one could touch her RRSP, pension, or savings. At the time, Steve was insulted by all of the banking bureaucracy.

"Didn't the doctor say to take it easy?"

Peg died five years ago. She loved tomatoes. Cooper never ate them, unless they were in a sauce. But he could tell you all the varieties: Beefeater, Roma, and Early Girl. He would stake them and prune the suckers. When the fruit came, he gave them a teaspoon of baking soda every other week. He continues to plant tomatoes but gives them to the neighbours. This year he'll grow lettuce, and with the right amount of rain and cool weather, it will thrive. Cooper doesn't like lettuce either and is only now learning the varieties: Counter, Grand Rapids, and May Queen.

"How's work?" Cooper asks.

"Mortgages, all day, every day. Everybody's buying. You have a corner lot. You should sell."

"I thought everyone's buying?"

Cooper was tired of his spiel, but he knew Steve was trying to cope, trying to right some wrong.

"If you want to stay longer, negotiate with the purchaser and rent," Steve says.

"We've talked about this. Why the hell would I rent my own house?"

"If you can get a good price."

"How much money do I really need?"

"Wasn't it supposed to be a starter home? You told Mom that."

Steam rises from the compost and Cooper gets back into the garden like he's stepping into a sauna. He takes up the hoe and chops at the soil, hilling it into rows. Turning it over, he spots a green-and-white shoot unfolding against the black husk of a peach pit. He drops the hoe, and scoops the pit up in both hands, carries it to the edge of the garden and drops it into a small clay pot. He adds more soil and gives it a splash from the watering can.

"Peaches in Surrey. We can dream, can't we? You know there's a seed vault in Norway. Built into the permafrost. There's an armed—."

Cooper leans on his shovel and turns to see his son sitting at the picnic table, thumb drumming his phone. He calls, "Hey! Stevie! Join me in the here and now!"

"Alright, take it easy."

He places his phone in his hip case.

"Remember that kickass tree fort? You and Timmy spent every day there that summer. I didn't say a word about the materials you took from the Super Value over on the King George, because I knew how much that fort meant to you. Besides they were small things. You have to pick your battles. Look at the bigger picture. And you turned out all right. I mean you never ended up in prison or in trouble with the law. Not like your little sister."

"I think her biggest crime was being unhappy."

Joanne's two years younger than Steve and enrolled in a mandatory drug and alcohol treatment program—part of her probation. Cooper gets the news second hand through Steve.

Cooper is convinced he let Steve get away with too much growing up. He was hard on Joanne. When she vomited in the kitchen sink and passed out on the linoleum after going to a friend's party, Cooper took away all her privileges, even though Steve had done the same thing many times. But after Peg passed away, Cooper caught Joanne in the woods by the house, plastic grocery bags at her feet, huffing Pam cooking spray. Now heroin is her drug. With it, she tries to create a different ending to what she witnessed, but can't stop. Survivor's guilt. The sound of heavy rain or a car engine triggers her flashbacks. Gone is the girl Cooper coached in inter-city soccer. The one who planted the potatoes and loved digging them up in the fall. His favourite picture is of her in the garden, holding a basket of those round brown beauties.

Cooper reaches for the small red cooler under the picnic table, flips the lid and pulls out a dripping bottle. He pins the cap against the tabletop and palm slams it. *Psssht.* He holds it out.

"Beer?"

The white suds trail across his fingers and down his arm, dripping onto the grass. There's a sweet fruity smell of home brew.

"No thanks. I'm on lunch."

"Have a beer for lunch."

Looking up, clutching the bottle against his forehead, Cooper says, "Notes of nuts and toffee, and a hoppy finish. I want one of those beer companies to write my eulogy."

Cooper takes a swig and lets out a burp.

About two months ago Cooper forgot the year he was born, and this set Steve off, so he started asking questions. Did Cooper ever forget where he parked the car? What month it was? Did he recognize the smell of a lemon?

"Have you given any more thought to Cherrington Place?"

"Hold on, Christ," Cooper scoffs. "Still alive over here. I'm not ready to give up on this."

Cooper spreads his arms, looking at the garden, the bird feeder and the apple tree. "A piece of paradise, if you ask me. And I may soon have a full-time helper."

A Darth Vader ringtone sounds. Steve smiles, raises an index finger, unsnaps his phone and faces the screen.

"I have to take this."

"Do those phones come in suppositories?"

Steve gets up from the table making a peace sign.

"Two minutes," he says and walks over to the woodpile. He talks and kicks at a piece of wood until it lines up with the others. He hangs up.

"My guys are coming to do the pool."

"Why do you have all that stuff if you can't take care of it? It's like you're paying other people to live your life."

"Cleaning a pool is not living life."

Steve tightens the knuckle on his tie.

"I have good news," Cooper says. "You know the Save-On-Foods? On Scott Road? Well, I met a woman there, a cashier. Her name is Alice. We've gotten to know each other pretty good in the past few months."

Cooper shopped in the early afternoon when the place was quiet. Under the buzz of fluorescents, music was pumped in from the store's sound system and cool air circulated from the frozen foods. All the ingredients were there. Wheeling his cart Cooper sang along to the "Sultans of Swing" by Dire Straits. He was the Sultan. Alice smiled when he arrived at the checkout. She pulled items from the conveyor, sliding the barcode over the scanner. *Ding. Ding.*

"Bags?"

"Normally I bring my own, but I left them on the kitchen counter."

"You should put them on the front seat. All that plastic in the food chain."

She counted out Cooper's change, touching his palm with a toonie.

They talked for longer when she worked the Deli counter.

"I'm from Winnipeg," she said, "so these winters are almost tropical."

She held up the cold cuts with gloved hands. "Thick enough?"

Cooper went for groceries, two, sometimes three times a day, until his fridge overflowed with milk and eggs. He tried to remember a time like this, when something this glorious got in, but he couldn't.

"So, it's serious then," Steve says.

"Yep. I guess."

Cooper reaches for the cooler and pulls out two sandwiches in Saran Wrap.

"Egg salad?"

Steve smiles and takes one, placing his phone on the table then peeling the wrapping off and crumpling it into a ball and tossing it into the cooler. Turning the sandwich on edge, he bites a corner, careful not to drop any of the fluffy filling on his suit. The homemade bread is fresh with a thick crust, the egg has bits of pickle that combine for a moist, tangy mouthful.

"Did you know," Steve asks, "that the smell of fresh bread makes us kinder to strangers?"

"Have you heard from your sister?"

"Sent me a text. She left Portage. Had a break from the program. She was at the Whalley station. Has a part-time job at a Garden Centre, working the nursery. She wanted me to make an e-Transfer, just to cover her until payday."

"Did you?"

"Are you crazy?"

Cooper tried having her live with him. She was high every night and lost the job at the Lumber Barn, the job he pulled strings for her to get. She stole his money, pawned his stereo. He had enough. He locked her out. He even called the cops when she tried to break in. Now he leaves the doors open in case she returns.

"It got bad after Mom died," Steve says. "Mom was her person."

"I just wasn't able to deal with her."

"Well, I need to go piss," Steve says, getting up and walking to the back entrance of the house.

Cooper pops the last bit of sandwich into his mouth and washes it down with the rest of his beer. He thinks about having another but decides not to. He's light-headed. His doctor told him to cut back on alcohol. He picks up a bottle cap from the lawn, snaps it back on the empty, and slides the bottle into the cooler.

"It's like it never happened," he says to no one.

He hears a bell and turns to see Alice resting her bicycle on the kickstand. Her blonde hair is twisted and tied into a single braid reaching the middle of her back, thick as a rope swing.

"Hello there," Alice says, walking to the picnic table. She spins Cooper's ball cap backward. "Hard at work? Or hardly working?"

"Lunch break, my dear. You want a drink? Sandwich—"

Steve's phone rattles loud on the table, with the "Imperial March." Cooper doesn't know what to do.

"Answer it," Alice says.

Turning it over, there is a picture of a girl, all pink cheeks and smiles. "It's Joanne." Cooper touches the green phone graphic. He hears her voice.

"Steve?"

"No, Jo. It's Dad."

"Oh?" She waits a second before speaking. "I guess you guys are great buddies now, hanging out on a weekday for some father-son time?"

"Yep, that's us."

"Tell me you're not letting that banker prick walk all over you. I want to hear it with my own ears. You were always such a fuck-up with money."

She's like a dog bark, in that quiet moment. Cooper's face pales. He grinds his teeth and all the regrets come up like oil on water. His heart rate quickens.

"Hey, Jo-Jo c'mon, I'm not interested in this right now. I wanna know how you are. I wanna know— "

"Sweep me under the rug, eh? Like some fucking abomination. I am not."

"Jesus, Jo, I know that." Cooper's breathing is all wrong, his voice cracks. "I know. I never thought that. None of us do. Listen to me—"

"Fuck you. You called the cops on me for trying to get into my own house. Asshole." *Click.*

Cooper places the phone back on the table, face down. He cups his chin and squishes his lips together.

"What is it?" Alice asks. "What did she say?"

A robin lands at the end of the picnic table, in the muted colours of the female. It looks at Cooper, flits its wings and takes off.

"Not sure."

Steve approaches, a red sweater in hand. When he was a baby, his mom would leave the sweater with him when he napped. "It has my scent sweetheart." A joke they shared. "Having trouble sleeping? I'll get the red sweater," or "Bad day at work? I'll get the red sweater."

Cooper doesn't notice it. "Alice, this is my son."

Alice reaches for Steve's hand. He switches the pile of red cloth to his left hand, and they shake.

"I'm taking this." Steve lifts the sweater.

"Wait, where was it?" Cooper asks.

"In a box by the door. Probably headed for the thrift shop. Can you check with me before you get rid of her...

her things? It's her birthday today. Did you remember that?"

There's a pause; a car horn blows.

"Take it," Cooper says.

"Alice, what brings you here?" Steve asks, rubbing his forehead.

"Making sure your father plants my lettuce and reminding him about bowling tonight."

"Bowling?" Steve says. "Sounds fun. Well, I have to get back to work. Thanks for the sandwich. We'll talk later. Nice to meet you."

"You should come with us," Alice says. "Scottsdale Lanes 7 p.m."

Cooper adds, "It's rude to turn down an invite, Stevie."

"Oh, Coop," Alice says. "Settle down."

Steve has decided to go. He's in the shoe line. He removes his brown leather slip-ons, licks his thumb, wipes some dust from the toe, and hands them over. Mel works the counter. He has a comb over, a small nameplate with *Manager* in cursive, and a belly that hangs over his belt. Steve, in socks, watches Mel place the blue-and-red bowlers on the counter.

"Why so ugly?" Steve says, pointing at the shoes.

"Accidental walkouts."

"Gotta be accidental, right?"

"I dunno," he shrugs. "It happens."

Mel gives each shoe a powdery aerosol blast.

"Your dad's a regular now. She has him filling out his score card every Wednesday night in the co-ed league."

"You know her?" Steve asks, reaching for his shoes.

Mel holds them in place. "I got a sister in Winnipeg. They were neighbours. I set her up with a job here. She's wonderful. It's her ex you have to watch out for."

"Ex?"

"Real nut job. Did some time at Stony Mountain. Domestic abuse, break and enter."

According to the police reports, Billie Jamieson would take Lori (that was her real name) for winter car rides, they would argue, and he would kick her out in minus 40, miles from the city, miles from anyone. A bus driver along that stretch picked her up more than once, half frozen. Then it was flowers and apologies, and he would sob when she packed to leave. If she walked to the car to leave, he would block the door. When she backed down the driveway, he knuckled the window, his voice muffled. "Don't do this to me. You want to fuck it all up?" She continued driving, increasing her speed, until he couldn't keep up, he hung from the sideview mirror, so heavy he broke it off, in a flash his palm squeaked across the glass, bright white skin, void of blood. Alice tapped the brakes. She couldn't do it, leave him, he'd rolled right into the ditch. When he saw her brake lights, a new belief burgeoned in Billie—it was her, she was the problem. The good news? She could fix this, if she really wanted to. "Please, don't press charges. I'm good. No more drinking, I promise. No more late nights. Besides, where would you go? What would you do when you get there?"

Mel lifts his hands from the shoes and nods. "Enjoy your game."

"Will do."

Steve slides his feet into the shoes and bends to recover the collapsed backs. When he tugs the laces, his hands shake.

Steve spots his dad and Alice in a high-back booth. People are everywhere, a windmill of arms, shuffles and slides. Some slap their thighs, others bump fists, or clap slow and loud, everything is moving left and right across the lanes, balls spinning and crashing into the pins.

They bowl for about an hour—enough time for two games. Alice describes the nursing program at Kwantlen College. One more semester and she begins a placement at the Royal Columbian Hospital. She starts in the Neonatal Intensive Care Unit, and then Emergency, followed by Geriatrics.

"Womb to tomb!" Alice laughs. "I get to see it all."

Before she gets up to take her turn, she rubs Cooper's shoulder.

"You hungry, Coop?" she asks then pulls out a Tupperware container of fruit.

"Dad tells me you're from Winnipeg," Steve says. "What's it like?"

Alice drops the fruit container, and two grapes roll under the computer console.

"Oh," she says picking up the fruit from the floor. "I'll need to wash these now."

"No, I got this. You stay."

Cooper picks up the fruit, places it back into the container and carries it over to the water fountain to rinse.

Steve stares at her like she's applying for a loan.

"What can I say? My marriage ended. I wanted out. Mel offered me a job. A chance to start over." Alice smiles. "And I met your father."

"How long were you married?"

"You're up, Stevie," Cooper says, returning with the fruit.

"Oh, right." He stands next to the ball return, grabs one and lines up his shot.

Alice leans into Cooper.

"You know," Alice says in a stage whisper, "I don't like these questions, it makes me nervous."

"He's curious, wants to get to know you."

Cooper watches Steve. His arm swings back. The weight of the ball is too much and, bringing it forward, he drops it too soon. *Crack*. It hits the hardwood and makes an early exit into the gutter.

"Lucky you get another shot," Cooper says.

When the game finishes Alice comes out on top with a score of 120.

They pick up their street shoes from the counter and head for the parking lot.

"Goodnight, Alice," Steve says. "Thanks for the invite."

Cooper takes Alice home, but before getting out of the truck she turns to him. "How do you feel about a baby?"

"A baby?" Cooper says, reaching up to scratch his head. "Alice, that's a big step."

Her demands build, one piling into another, like floating ice when a river narrows. And all of it on Peg's birthday. Cooper switches off the heater and adjusts the rear-view mirror. He sees a cigarette glow and hears someone start a car.

"I better head home," Cooper says. "We'll talk more tomorrow."

Cooper pulls into his driveway. The bathroom light is on. "Probably just forgot to turn it off." He takes the key from the ignition and walks in the front door. He hears a toilet and the sound of water travelling the pipes. The bathroom door opens and floorboards creak from the weight of someone else.

"Hello? Stevie? That you?" Cooper calls out. "Let me guess, you have documents for me to sign."

No response.

He sees the outline of an unfamiliar man. His moves quicken Cooper's heart rate.

"You don't know me," the stranger says, "but I recognize you."

His pointed finger moves in time with his words, and he smiles, proud of his discovery. "From one picture on Lori's Facebook page. She's Alice to you."

The room is dim with only light from the street. The man is wearing an orange puffer jacket, and grey sweats with an Edmonton Oilers logo on the thigh. The jacket makes him look bigger than he is. He's bearded, his head wrapped snug in a hood, draw strings pulled tight.

"What the hell are you doing in here?" Cooper asks.

"If you only knew how many times people ask me that. Such a stupid question. I mean, think about it. What sort of answer are you hopin' for?"

"This is my home." Cooper takes a step back. "Get out!"

"Not so fast. Lower your voice, old man."

He pushes Cooper into the recliner, grabs hold of his arm, lifting him slightly from the chair and jerking him back and forth.

"Listen close, you little fucker. I want you to keep away from Lori. Got it?"

"Dad?" A voice calls from the back entrance. "You home? You're letting out all of the bought air!" Joanne says laughing, closing the door behind her.

"Jo, that you? In the living room. In some trouble here."

Joanne clicks the switch. The man lets go of Cooper.

Joanne's skin is white and flaky, like pastry, and an open sore weeps under one eye.

"Who the fuck—?" Joanne moves in, grabs the man's throat and digs in with her nails, crumpling his skin into her fist like a piece of paper. Driving forward she pushes him over Cooper's outstretched legs. The man grabs a handful of Joanne's hair as he falls, pulling her head down so it bounces off the floor. He rolls to his side, stands and runs out the front door.

Silence fills the room. The kind that makes you feel like the only survivor.

Then rain comes down in great drops that shake the house, spilling out of the gutters into downspouts and ditches: more water than space to contain it. A gust of cool air blasts the front door shut. *Whack.*

Cooper remembers the heavy rain that night, too. Peg was driving with Joanne in the passenger seat. They took Highway 91 headed for False Creek, the quickest route at that time of night. According to Joanne, Peg found the steering wheel tough to turn. Off went the radio.

"What is it?" Jo had asked.

The rhythmic thump was getting louder.

"Flat," her mom said, pulling onto the shoulder before the Alex Fraser Bridge.

Never get out! Cooper remembers the public service announcements. *Call from inside and arrive alive.* But

Peg stepped onto the asphalt, two feet from a live lane and cars whizzing by like bullets. The 18-wheeler strayed. The rumble strips did not rouse the driver. The rig struck Peg at 118 km/h, enough speed and weight to sheer the door off, like plucking a wing from an insect.

Right now, Joanne is on the floor with a clump of hair and skin beside her on the carpet. Cooper supports her neck and thighs as he lifts, so thin and light—she's bird-like. When she was a girl, he often carried her asleep from the car, just like this. He sets her in the recliner and lowers the back to raise the front. Her hand falls from the armrest and hangs motionless, dark soil wedged beneath her nails. Her eyes dart under the lids, she breathes and mumbles nonsense.

THE QUESTIONS RUN

JAMES SELLERS AND Peter Segaros sit in class and think: In fifteen minutes we'll be high. At least that's the plan. It's a month after Ozzy Osbourne bit the head off a bat, and everyone, well, mostly the boys, are in basements, smoking pot, listening to "Stairway to Heaven" and trying to spot the phrase, "Here's to my sweet Satan." You hear it when you reverse the spin of the record, playing the song the opposite way; backmasking, when a message is recorded backward on a track, meant to be played forward. When Peter and James found it, they felt like the archaeologists who unearthed the Rosetta stone. What message is backmasking their lives—that others hear, but they can't?

Two weeks ago, Peter and James took some cash to the Mac's Milk parking lot. Peter stood beside a garbage dumpster, and lit a smoke, the universal signal. And they waited. The dealers always found them. A lowered green Datsun, one they had never seen before, pulled in with a C-Fox sticker in the window, feather roach clips hanging from the rear view, and primed grey fenders. The power chords from "Iron Man" rattled all the metal on the car, making every strum, every drum beat longer. James stepped closer to Peter.

"Relax, Sellers," Peter said. "And hold this," handing James his smoke. "We're buyers."

Killing the music, the dealer got out, leaving the driver's door open. He had a silver cross in his left ear and a storm rider jean jacket with an Iron Maiden *Number of the Beast* back patch. On it, Eddie's a master puppeteer, dancing the Devil on strings, who in turn dances some guy further below. The allusion is clear—someone controls everyone. During a one-armed hug the dealer slipped the weed into Peter's jacket pocket, then went into Mac's. Coming out, he gave James a slush cat and Peter a hoagie, then collected the cash, as though this exchange protected him from prosecution.

The dealer pulled away. Peter peeled off the plastic wrap, and bit into the thinly sliced ham, salami, and cheese, a glob of Italian dressing glistened on his chin. "This is fucking good. Try some."

"Swamp mix," James said, swirling the contents before he exchanged it for the sandwich. "That guy's raking it in." He watched the dealer's Datsun zip from Mac's to the Safeway parking lot and took a bite of the sandwich.

"Yeah," Peter's mouth hung open, handing the slush cat back to James. "I bet he covers the 7-Eleven on Scott Road and the Whalley one. I'd only need a car."

"And a driver's license." James emptied the slush cat, gurgled through the last of it with loud draws of air, and tossed the cup into the dumpster. "Are you for real?"

"Fuck the paper route. And why cut grass when I can sell it?"

Peter didn't really know what would come of that, but James did.

"Hey, steer clear of that shit."

Peter wanted the sandwich back, but James held it out of reach. "I'm serious."

James didn't want to mention Peter's mom, didn't want to have to remind him of her.

Right now, back in class, the bag of weed is tucked into the mickey pocket of Peter's gold and black Newton minor hockey jacket with *Staff* stitched onto the sleeve. His cuffed Big Blue jeans drape his faded green Stan Smiths. He never takes that jacket off. He sleeps in it.

Peter's the only one who can roll a joint. And maybe he felt so far behind the other kids, so far down that hill, that he wanted to go the other direction. Getting up from his desk, he gives James the double eyebrow lift. Where can you roll without getting caught? Some place without wind or rain, or a parent's prying eyes or a little sister who sneaks up and asks, "Whatcha doin'?" The Georges Vanier Elementary boys' bathroom. On his way out of class, he flipped the laminated bathroom wall key from green to red. Only one student left at a time, and often it was Peter. That laminated key might as well have read, *Get me outta here!*

Waiting at the fountain, he checks the empty hallway. A quiet exists in this space between the classrooms and the outside world. A buffer from the pressure to learn, to get it all in, day after day in a kind of educational arms race on one side, his family on the other. Peter's family is really only his dad, and his half-assed attempts to be present. His mom is absent, incarcerated in the Fraser Valley on a four-year bit for drug possession. And there's Stella, his five-year-old sister always asking, "when's Mama home for good?"

Peter looks for Mr. Forcier, the principal, but chances are he's in his office before lunch supervision.

Peter twists the fountain handle and watches water arc from the silver spigot to the drain, then cuts it off with three big gulps. He swipes his jacket cuff across his mouth, darkening the black satin fabric. Opening the bathroom door to the bright smell of lemon, he catches his mirror image, stops, adjusts his jacket, and shakes hair over his eyes. In the stall, he lowers the lid and sits on the throne, listening to the water trickle from the cistern to the urinals. All of it flowing out to sea, the good, the bad, the final destination. Then what happens? He lays down the weed and the Zig-Zags on top of the toilet paper dispenser. Moving slowly, he tugs a rolling paper free from the pack, and holds it open between his finger and thumb, sprinkling in some pot, he rolls it back and forth with both hands, increasing the pressure. The tighter the roll, the longer the burn.

A hinge squeaks.

Peter freezes. He listens for the next sound. *Shit.* He knows Mr. Forcier's walk and the worn brown leather shoes that squeak the tile floor turning to face him below the stall door. Holding the joint to his mouth, Peter's tongue darts out to lick the gummy end of the paper to finish.

In class, James waits for Peter to roll and swears to God someone hung that clock at the front as torture. Where the hell is he? His eyes shift from Mrs. Charlebois to the clock, like a human second hand. The real second-hand glides over large black numbers, the word *SIMPLEX* dead centre—but that hour hand never moves, or at least he never sees it. Might as well snap it off. Maybe it mirrors school, how the fifteen-minute recess blows by, but when Mrs. Charlebois tells them, "Writing was invented in Mesopotamia," trying to hammer home the significance of it all, his eyes go straight to the hour hand. He couldn't give a shit about Mesopotamia, but her voice just won't let it go and it blends in with the low-pitched buzz of fluorescents. Forget water boarding, her voice is like some kind of ether-induced coma.

"Stella Segaros please report to the office," comes from the intercom. "Stella Segaros to the office."

Stella, Peter's little sister, called to the office. James wonders if letting Peter hold the stuff was a good idea. He's a magnet. He's on that troubled kid map drawn up by the ones in power—parents and teachers—the gatekeepers. A map of the valued and the not-so-valued. The future athlete, the honours English and math student, or the coveted science whiz: have you considered putting that talent to use? They're gonna need people like you in the room to make the important decisions. No need to decide now but keep it in your back pocket. Think it over. The not-so-valued aren't so lucky, it's eye rolls and deep sighs, it's hands thrown in the air in the middle of long division, and Mrs. Charlebois blurting to Peter, "You couldn't find your ass with both hands." It's the rest of us.

James knows Grade Three show-and-tell landed Peter on that troubled kid map when Mrs. Garries pointed to the masking tape *X* at the front of the room like a stewardess identifying the emergency exit. Peter was held back, so he was big, even then, with long, loping strides, and brown curls that swayed with each desk weave.

"All right, Peter," Mrs. Garries had said with Peter in position, "whenever you're ready."

Then she retreated to the chair behind her desk.

Up there, most kids were nervous and looked at the carpet, wringing their hands. But not Peter. Once he had your gaze, he didn't break it.

"My mom was home for the weekend and she caught me smoking."

After he said it, he stepped back, freed his thumb from a belt loop and pushed his wrist into his groin to adjust.

That was Peter's go-to move when he had something exciting to share. James put down his pencil crayon because in the spotlight, Peter rarely disappointed. And there he was, in front of the class talking about smoking.

"She gave me a full pack and told me I had to smoke 'em all, right there, right now. 'All of 'em, Peter!'" He smiled with one side of his mouth.

He pushed his groin again. "So I smoked." He made a peace sign and touched his fingers to his lips. "Twenty-five." He pretended to blow rings... you could almost see smoke floating above his head.

Peter smiled at Mrs. Garries, but when he turned back to the class, he was pale, and pain took over. With a hand on his stomach and puffed cheeks, he sprayed a thick puke stream onto the carpet. It was followed by a loud gasp from the kids, and panic. Some stood; others crashed their chairs into desks, all to avoid the splash. It didn't phase Peter, it couldn't, he convulsed again and again, and his projectile vomiting would not stop. The boys sat and watched him suffer.

Mrs. Garries carried the garbage can over to Peter like a shield.

"Oh, Peter," she said, "some memories aren't so good."

She didn't catch a drop. Puke splashed the wall below the chalkboard, spotting the class Valentine's Day projects. And even though the janitor shuffled in later, sprinkled sawdust and shovelled up the puke piles—that sour smell never left the classroom. It was something that stayed.

Teachers shared that show-and-tell smoking story like it was a public service announcement, and Peter would finally get the help he needed. But the effect was the opposite. Peter was given all the special jobs, like he was being groomed for something blue-collar, something skilled-trades. He ran the projector, fixing film that ran off the guides, or remounted a loose reel. Trusted to hold the ladder when Mr. Forcier went on the school roof to get the soccer balls. Kids idolized Peter, like some kind of rock star—the principal's right-hand man. But Peter was given those roles as a means of control: to keep him close; to burden him with responsibility.

During the Eggstravaganza science competition, students designed a container to protect an egg dropping thirty feet from the primary play area roof to the tarp-covered gravel below. Peter was on the roof with Mr. Forcier. The rise to stardom complete. He passed each project to Mr. Forcier, who announced the design team before dropping them to student cheers. If yolk oozed from the tangle of Styrofoam, wooden spokes, and carpet tape, the kids booed.

What Mr. Forcier didn't notice was this: on Fridays Peter removed the basement key from the master set. The underground space was cold, cobweb-filled and lit by a single pull-string bulb. On Saturday nights, with James on lookout, Peter moved from the storage shelves he helped to fill, to the wide-open area beyond, flicking his BiC lighter when it got dark. There is a thrill in darkness, when your bearings are gone but you still have to keep moving to get out of it. Crawling on the concrete in places, Peter made it to a trap door below the auxiliary lady's lunchroom where they stored the hot dog and hamburger day snacks. He took Hostess chips, BBQ peanuts, and hulled, roasted sunflower seeds, sliding a filled box ahead in the spaces he had to crawl. He didn't celebrate hot dog and hamburger day like the other kids: that excitement they felt when their name was followed by "two hot dogs with ketchup and mustard," "one hamburger with ketchup and mustard," "a bag of salt and vinegar chips, and two Cokes." Still, on some mornings Peter did have ketchup sandwiches for lunch, if he found bread in the house.

He delivered the orders to all the classes. Over and over, he watched those kids walk up and lift their food from that blue laundry basket and into their mouths, and it helped him crawl to that trap door. Depending on the inventory, some weekends he swiped entire flats of Coke and Sprite. Every time he did it, James was on lookout, but refused to go in, using this as evidence he did nothing wrong. He was not an accomplice. With the snack inventory dropping, the school administration wised-up, and installed magnetic contacts on all the doors.

On the final raid, when James heard tires on gravel, car doors open and close and the quick steps of the RCMP, he leaned into the basement and yelled, "Cops!" because he knew that nothing gets better when the cops show up. James ran hell-bent to the woods on the edge of the soccer field. Peter couldn't make it out, so he stayed and moved into a dusky basement corner. What did they want from Peter? Didn't they know he had no other way to get those things? No other way to feel like the other kids. His face was hidden when the flashlight beams searched the crawl space. Peter listened to every creak and faint word between the officers for the word *dog* or any dog sounds, because that would be the end. More time passed and Peter knew that he couldn't leave. He stayed all night, curled up in that corner, and froze his ass off. When first light appeared under the basement door, he crawled back with that full box and turned the handle from the inside to get out.

With a slick of dew on the grass and the sun's orange glow warming his face and hands, Peter walked home. A long silver cobweb trailed his elbow as he passed Mrs. Jenkins, a neighbour out walking her dog. "Burning the candle at both ends eh, Peter?"

"Better to burn it out," Peter replied, tipping the last sunflower seeds into his mouth, and dropped the bag on the sidewalk, "than fade away."

"Peter?" Mr. Forcier asks, standing at the bathroom stall. "You in there?"

"Yessir," he says, carefully swiping everything into the baggie and sliding it back into his mickey pocket.

"It's your father, there's been an accident at the mill. I'm about to call Stella down to the office."

The thought of Stella, waiting alone at the office, afraid and full of questions, makes his arm hairs stand. Peter buttons his jacket all the way up, pushing his hair over his ears. The questions run for him, too—what happened? Is he okay? Why are you calling us both down? His father's part of the fire crew. The chip silos do catch fire, Peter knows that, but it's a slow, smouldering burn, like a pile of damp leaves. Not a searing cauldron so hot it turns a body to ash. His dad often came home smelling of cedar smoke and Captain Morgan. "My job at the mill," his dad would say tangled in a laugh, "is what I do between drinks." But he always came home.

Peter stands, flushes the toilet, and clears his throat, "Be right out, Mr. Forcier."

The clock hands reach straight up in a sign of surrender, and the lunch bell rings. James knows this day will no longer be extraordinary. Peter never came back to class. James walks to the library window to get a clear look at the pickup and drop-off zone. Peter and Stella are there; his hand rests atop her head. A police car pulls in, an officer gets out in a tan shirt, adjusting his gold-striped black cap to cover his eyes. He opens the passenger door and motions for Stella to get in.

James slides the library window open, sticks his head out and yells, "Hey, Pete!"

Peter sees James in his yellow Georges Vanier T-shirt, an eagle emblazoned across the chest, and flips him the finger with both hands.

"Yeah, fuck you, Peter!" James laugh-yells back. "Fuck you, too!"

"James Sellers! Language!" comes from the librarian Mrs. Livingstone standing behind him. "Close that window and get outside for lunch!"

James doesn't move. He watches Peter duck into the back of the cop car. What difference does it make? He feels like they took Peter away long before that cop car arrived.

Later James found out that Peter was separated from Stella and relocated to a new school. A motherless and fatherless family broken, crumbled into smaller bits, and swiped to the floor.

"Yeah," James says to Mrs. Livingstone. "I'm goin'."

James walks back to his locker and finds a bag of weed on the top shelf, a joint visible through the plastic.

ACKNOWLEDGEMENTS

Some of these stories have previously appeared in magazines or contests: "The Questions Run" was an honourable mention in the 2025 Riddle Fence Fiction Contest and was subsequently published in *Riddle Fence*; "Until Someone is Named" in *The Miracle Monocle*; "Powderman" in *Canadian Shorts II* and *The Impressment Gang*; "The Weight of Someone Else" in *QWERTY*; "Blowing Across the Top" in Literally Stories; "All the Little Things" in *Just Words Vol 3* and *Blank Spaces*; "Starting People" and "Falling" in *The Nashwaak Review;* "Forbidden Spaces" in *Impressment Gang*; and "Trace" in *Grain Magazine*. I am grateful to all of the editors of these literary magazines—Stewart Donovan, Adam Pottle, Pearl Chan, Alanna Rusnak, Leila Allison, Lauren R. Korn, Brenda Fisk, Sara Strickley, and Carmella Gray-Cosgrove. For many writers, you are the starting point.

I am deeply grateful to my editors Linda Leith and Felicia Mihali at Linda Leith Publishing for their interest in the manuscript and subsequent expertise, guidance, and support during publication. Shakiya Williams for keeping me on track. Robert Edison Sandiford reviewed an early draft of the manuscript. His support and expertise were both timely and motivating. Harold Hoefle has been a mentor throughout the writing process; right down there in the muck of it, his editorial feedback is invaluable. Thank you, my friend. I am deeply indebted to you for your generosity of time and spirit. André LeBlanc (ECE), and first reader, you have read them all. Your willingness to question, challenge, and contemplate the big ideas knows no bounds, and for that I am grateful. Claire Russell generously provided her thoughtful feedback on many of these stories, helping me grow and refine my craft as a writer.

Victor Rose, for a cozy chair, half-sweet mocha, and just the right amount of background noise.

A big thank you to the Foys—my brother Andrew, his wife Teresa, and children Jordan, Conlan, Carson, and Avery. Your dad is in many of these stories; look closely, he's there.

Oma and Opa, for asking, "How's the writing going?"

Krista, my wife, and our daughters, Addison and Paige, all the best things in my life come from you three. Krista, I would like to especially acknowledge you for helping to finance all of those coffee house trips and lending an ear and a critical eye when I need it most. Sometimes I get lost out there, but you help me find a way home.

AVAILABLE AND COMING SOON FROM
LINDA LEITH PUBLISHING

Linda Leith Publishing is a Canadian literary press founded in 2011.

Our mission is to publish and promote exceptional literary work by Canadian writers and translators that engages with the changes in the worlds we inhabit. Based in Montreal, we are always on the lookout for new voices and new talent.

We, the Others
TOULA DRIMONIS

The Language of the Stars
NATHAN HELLNER-MESTELMAN

Here Is Still Here
SIVAN SLAPAK

Other Maps
REBECCA MORRIS

The Bigamist
FELICIA MIHALI

Miss Matty
EDEET RAVEL

Sentence
Mickail Iossel

Christmas Weekend
Monique Polack

The Unfinished World
Marilyn Bowering

There's Always More to Say
Natalie Southworth

I Made a Promise I Could not Keep
David Homel

Beyond Ken Dryden
Oren Safdie

I Can't Believe I'm Old
Janet Torge

The Roughling
Alex Costa

The Faithful
Don Macdonald

FSC
www.fsc.org
MIX
Paper
FSC® C100212

Printed by Imprimerie Gauvin
Gatineau, Québec